CAPTAIN
OF THE
MONTE CRISTO

JOHN GUNNINGHAM
&
SARAH K. L. WILSON

To My Family
-John Gunningham

For Scotland, because I wouldn't know
anything about gaming if he wasn't my brother.
-Sarah K. L. Wilson

CHAPTER : 1

S corched circuits and the tang of human blood were all Lieutenant Edmond Dante could smell as he clung to the grips on his command chair.

"Helm, turn her two-point-five-four degrees. Alpha missiles launch on my mark. Five, four, three, two, launch!"

Dante's holoscreen showed the missiles screaming into the pirate ship, but the *Dauntless* was already floundering under the pummeling she'd received.

"Helm is sluggish, Lieutenant." Rogers' tone was tight as he worked the data streams coming from the helm.

Edmond swallowed hard. The Captain had come in fat and lazy on a predictable sector approach and this is what had greeted them: pirates. He should have known, but there was no time to think of that now.

"Incoming at a vector of zero-point-nine-two."

"Evasive maneuvers, deploy counter-missiles!" he barked, but their ship was already bucking under enemy fire multiple soundless firecrackers in the vacuum of space. Clouds of gas streamed from the punctures in the hull before the auto repair systems could seal off damaged sectors.

"We've done all we can, they're still closing. They'll be boarding us soon."

Edmond struck the arm of the command chair hard with his fist before he glanced at the pale Captain as the medical officer, Mercedes, did her best to stop him from drowning in his own blood. The ship's engineer, Fernand, frantically tried to get his attention over Edmond's implanted comm unit.

"Edmond, they're hailing us," he said urgently in the Lieutenant's. "You need to come to engineering."

"One moment," Edmond said, putting his finger to his jaw to speak to Fernand before dropping to his knees beside Mercedes. "Will he make it?"

She wiped the sweat on her forehead, heedless of the blood she smeared there. She was working on the floor where the Captain had fallen with her kit spread out beside her.

"I don't know. If that first salvo hadn't ruined my medical station, I'd say yes without a doubt. With only three field kits, though..." her voice trailed off. "He needs a real medical center, but I'll do what I can," she finished firmly.

"I know you will—you always do." There was no time for the embrace Dante wanted to give her, but he prayed there would be time later. He clasped her shoulder instead.

"Edmond, they're coming, damn you! The Captain can die well enough without your company!" Fernand insisted.
Dante found his fist clenched tight and forced himself to loosen it. Fernand was not wrong, despite his lack of tact.

"Coming," he said over the comm.

"Be safe," Mercedes said. Her eyes spoke volumes before she turned back to her work.

Dante nodded once and then was off, hurtling through the narrow corridors of the ship. It was a short way to go; the emergency protocols had locked down a large portion of the habitable space as soon as the first cannon had been fired. It was only good fortune that none of the crew had been blown into space outright. It had been poor fortune that shrapnel had found the Captain as he'd rushed to sound general quarters.

He again felt his anger rising as he passed the damage. These pirates would pay!

"There you are, and nearly late!" Fernand looked up from his holographic data stream. He was uncharacteristically filthy, having had to perform emergency repairs manually, as several of the ship's self-maintenance protocols had failed. He wore a bulky atmosphere suit with the helmet's visor pushed up as he gestured to the hatch in front of him. "They're forcing their way in here, I'm sure of it. They've already attached their ship's docking mechanism—I saw that much before the cameras went dead. Here, you'll need a suit." Fernand pulled one from the rack and thrust it at Dante.

"You think they'll vent the air? Kill us all?" He struggled into the space suit even as he heard the hard, metallic sounds of tools forcing entry into their ship and violating her locks.

"Oh, I doubt that's their intention, but it is mine." Fernand brandished his fist inside the data stream with an evil grin. "When they connected with us, I managed to get inside them."

"You've taken control of their ship?"

"I'm an engineer, Dante, not a hacker, but I was able to gain access to their environmental controls." Fernand pulled his helmet down and his voice took on the filtered sound of all electronic communication. "It's about to get very cold for our pirate friends."

"You'll kill them!" Dante exclaimed.

"That's the point. Better them than us," Fernand said. "I thought seeing the Captain would have made that extremely clear. These men will kill us for our cargo without a second thought. Think of yourself, man. Think of Mercedes!"

"Think of your conscience!" the Edmond countered. They couldn't be having this conversation! "You're talking about mass murder!"

"In self-defense," Fernand said with a shrug. Ahead of them, the door creaked and groaned. The pirate boarding party was nearly through. "Get your suit and let's finish this quickly."

"This is wrong and you know it," Dante said firmly. "I can't condone it!"
He looked Fernand in the eye as he deliberately set his helmet on the floor.

"If you go through with it, it will be my life with theirs." He was proud that his voice didn't waiver much when he spoke. "I won't allow any such actions until we've exhausted negotiations."

Fernand stared blankly as the locked door lost the last of its resolve and was pushed inward by three men and a woman wearing mismatched gear. They carried weapons which looked to be in poor repair. Dante stood firm and exposed.

"Ah, you've saved us the trouble of finding you," the first man said over the built-in speakers in his suit. He didn't remove his helmet or show his face, but his voice had the resignation of an older man.

"We're here to accept the terms of your surrender," Edmond responded, trying to sound like he was in command.

9

"Well, look at the balls of brass on this one, eh, lads?" the pirate boomed. "Full points for bravado, boy, but you're in no position to make demands. We'll be the ones taking your surrender," he laughed as their weapons were primed and pointed.

"Listen carefully, because I will only say this once: we've gained access to your environmental controls and can vent your ship's atmosphere whenever we choose," Dante said. "Now, throw down your weapons and surrender your ship."

Please listen to reason. No one else needs to die here.

"You're bluffing," the pirate said in disdain after a moment of reflection.

"Not at all," Fernand said, stepping closer. He keyed a quick sequence in his data stream and smiled like a fox. The boarding party responded almost instantly to what must have been an outburst on their comm channel.

"Only enough for a show of force, Fernand, nothing more," Edmond said quietly. "I beg you." The Lieutenant couldn't be sure, but he thought he felt the air grow thin, even here.

"Of course," the engineer said, tapping his controls again. "Only enough for a scare."

"Still think we're bluffing?" Dante called out.

In response, the boarding party tossed their weapons aside and showed their empty hands.

CHAPTER : 2

"It was enough that we threatened them!" Edmond said again as he paced back and forth on the deck of the officer's mess where Edmond had called the meeting of officers.

"It would have been better to just flush the atmosphere. Now we have a ship of pirates to deal with—to feed and police." Fernand carefully dragged a hand through his hair, trying not to muss it too much. Edmond frowned. Was Fernand so much of a peacock that he cared what his hair looked like at a time like this? "We don't have the space to keep them all, and with a second ship to pilot as a prize we'll need to split off crew to cover her stations. If we didn't have prisoners, this wouldn't be a problem. You haven't been down there, trying to repair the automated systems, like I have. We were almost destroyed in the attack!"

"Could we cannibalize the pirate's ship for parts and leave her here?" Edmond said, looking out through the officer's mess window at their prize. Her running lights were lit at regular intervals along her hull; for a pirate's rig, she was well-built and maintained. "Either way, we must make our decision quickly. The Captain won't last much longer."

"We can't leave the ship," Villefort, the ship's purser, spoke for the first time since they'd shut themselves away from the crew. "If it's a choice

12

between the prize and the pirates, it must be the prize. We all have the debts of our commissions to pay, and the prize will almost cover those."

Edmond grunted. Of course the purser was worried about money.

"Grunt all you want, Edmond. Some of us want to buy back our indentures." Villefort said.

"Some of us have a few extra debts to settle, eh Villefort?" Fernand nudged him with an elbow. Edmond frowned as Villefort brushed Fernand's elbow away. It was no secret that he was hilt-deep in debt. Was that clouding his judgment? Surely, they couldn't both be heartless enough to see their fellow men flushed out the air locker.

"Regardless, our employers will not be pleased if we lose the ship."

"It's worse to lose the lives of the men who crewed her," Edmond said, rubbing his chin.

"They're pirates, Edmond—the company might even praise us for ridding space of the vermin," Fernand stood and stretched his back. "They're criminals—human trash—and your ridiculous sympathies are wasted on them. My vote is to send them out the airlock. It's an easy, cheap solution. We can then check in at the closest planet and get the old man some medical care."

"Captain Moreau can't go to the nearest planet. None of us can. It's Elba. You know who's there… and

13

why. Just entering orbit is almost enough to be accused of treason." Villefort sounded aghast.

"Medical Bay to First Officer," the overhead comm chirped.

"First Officer," Edmond responded, holding his finger to his jaw bone. The implanted mic read his sub-vocalizations and needed no assistance, but he'd never been able to shake the feeling that holding his finger there made it clearer.

"Edmond, we need to get Captain Moreau to a full medical facility as soon as possible. Where are we on that?" Mercedes' voice was tight on the comm.

"Working on it."

"Work faster!"

"How long can you keep him stable?"

"The nearest planet might not be close enough, but we'd better head there now. Edmond," she paused, her voice hushed, "he's hemorrhaging to death."

"The closest planet is Elba, Mercedes."

"I don't care if it's Hell. If you want him to live, you'll take us there."

An alarm whooped in the medical bay and her signal cut off. Edmond rubbed his forehead. What to do? Going to Elba was close to treason, but the Captain's life hung in the balance. If only he hadn't been suckered by the pirates.

"Is the medial station in the pirate ship working?" he suddenly asked.

"Negative—it's as trashed as ours. If we go to Elba, we definitely shouldn't take the pirates," Fernand said. "Mercedes' diagnosis settles it. I vote we get rid of them."

"Get rid of them?" Edmond asked, "Like bed bugs? They're people! I vote we turn them in to the authorities. We'll go to Elba for the Captain and we can turn the pirates in to the garrison there."
Fernand's jaw clenched stubbornly, and Edmond turned on his last potential ally.

"Tell him, Villefort! Tell him we can't just kill people!"

Villefort tapped the table with his fingers. "What about the ship? Our prize?"

"If I promise to find a way to keep them both, will you agree to my plan?" Why couldn't they see how inhumane they were?

Villefort hesitated.

"Oh, for crying out loud, Edmond!" Fernand's expression was all hard lines and frustration. "You'd risk treason and mutiny just to salve your precious honor?"

"You'll keep the prize and we'll sell it?" Villefort verified.

"Yes! How many times must I say it?" Edmond asked. If only he could pull rank. The regulations, however, were specific that, in a crisis of leadership, he needed a quorum of the surviving officers.

15

"I'll vote with you, then."

"I won't set foot on that ship," Fernand said, "and I won't serve brig duty. If you do this, you do it on your own."

"You won't have to," Edmond said. "I'll brig them on their own ship and crew it myself. We can tow our ship with theirs, slave the computers, and pilot them in tandem from *Dauntless*. I'll be the only one at risk. If there are any problems, you can cut me off and leave."

"That means I'll be piloting both ships," Fernand said with a smile on his lips. "You have that much faith in me?"

Edmond nodded, "I do. Get us there safely and quickly. You heard Mercedes: the Captain's life depends on it."

He slapped the door release panel and waited for the locks to withdraw. He'd brokered a deal for the pirates' lives, but could he pull it off? Crewing a ship using captives wasn't going to be easy – especially out here in the boundary planets. They were lush, to be certain, but the law barely reached them, and there would be no one to call on for help if violence broke out again.

Fernand laughed. "Don't worry about me— worry about yourself. If your new friends mutiny over there, I'll flush the breathable air... whether *you're* suited up or not."

"I'd expect nothing less, Fernand."

16

"Medical Bay to First Officer."

"Edmond," Mercedes' voice was even tighter, "are we moving yet?"

He had to hurry—she wouldn't sound so raw if she wasn't afraid of losing a patient.

CHAPTER : 3

Edmond watched the blue and green planet come into view with an involuntary shudder—and he wasn't the only one.

"I've heard stories of Elba," the young pirate handcuffed to the co-pilot's chair next to Edmond said. "None of them end well for anyone."

Edmond pursed his lips. "You don't know the half of it," he murmured as he glanced at the boy. He's so young. Pirating must be all he knows.

"Jack, right?"

The boy nodded without taking his eyes off the planet below.

"Normally I wouldn't condemn anyone here—not even pirates—but we have no choice. It was this or a short walk out an airlock. Do you understand?"

Jack didn't say anything as he stared at the planet with what must have been a thousand stories of infamy running through his head. Edmond scrubbed his hands over his tired eyes. Well, this was what happened to pirates, wasn't it? Surely being incarcerated was better than death. Edmond tried to clear the thoughts from his mind, as there were other important matters to attend to.

He steeled his resolve and opened a channel to Elba.

"This is Company ship 60-215 *Dauntless* requesting clearance to land. We have a medical emergency and require immediate aid." For a moment, there was no response. He repeated himself into the abyss. Did the planet lack basic communication as part of its quarantine protocol? It took another tense minute for a reply to come.

"*Dauntless,* you are in direct violation of Company directive and quarantine protocols by communicating with this planet. Do you understand?"

He closed his eyes, memories of the Captain and all his mercy flooding through his mind.

"The man asks a good question," Jack muttered beside him. "You better have a damn good answer, for all our sakes."

While looking at the frank pirate boy, Edmond spoke to the official, "Understood. I repeat, we have a medical emergency and require immediate medical attention. It must be Elba—we haven't the time to go anywhere else. We have also taken prisoner a complement of pirates. We wish to transfer the custody of them and their ship to you, as per regulation."

"Very well, so long as you understand the risks." The voice on the other end of the conversation went dead, but the ship's computers were already being fed instructions, and, for good or ill, they were beginning to enter Elba's orbit. "We'll send a shuttle for you and your wounded, as well as inform the Marines of your pirate problem. You'll need to report to the surface. This is not an option."

"For the record, I was against all of this," Fernand said from the *Dauntless,* his voice sudden in Edmond's ear.

He smiled. "When will you learn to trust me, Fernand?"

"You have the Devil's own luck, I'll give you that," Fernand said, "but I've learned you can't always trust in luck and good fortune. At some point, you need to make your own way."

"I am, for the Captain's sake," Edmond said before cutting the communications channel to the *Dauntless.* He put his head in his hands. He's not wrong. No matter, they were committed to this course. No matter what might be ahead for all of them, Edmond felt relief from having chosen a path. He shook his head, trying to dislodge the weariness that fogged his thoughts.

"Is your captain really so critical that Elba is his only chance?" Jack asked.

Edmond looked up at the young pirate. "Yes, because of you and your crew," he said. "The first salvo sent shrapnel into him, as well as destroyed our medical bay."

Jack was quiet a moment. "That wasn't supposed to happen."

Anger welled up and Edmond couldn't trust himself to speak for a moment. He was glad when he felt a familiar presence enter the cockpit behind him.

"Fernand told me we've gained access to Elba," Mercedes said as she crouched next to Edmond's chair.

"It's easier to land than to leave," Edmond said, shaking his head. "The Captain?"

"I've done what I can. He's stable, but not for long. I only hope he can survive planet fall."

"He has to, for us to risk this much. He has to," Edmond said before taking a deep breath and smiling. "We only need to have faith."

The doctor's shoulders slumped with exhaustion, but she smiled and rested her head on Edmond's shoulder. "You always expect the best. It's the most frustrating and wonderful thing about you."

"I heard he was debating blowing us out an airlock to save feeding us," Jack said. "He doesn't seem too wonderful to me."

Mercedes glared at the boy, her lips thinning. "Edmond saved your worthless pirate life.

21

Despite all reason and sound argument, you will survive to stand trial when we return."

"Mercedes…" Edmond began.

"No, you're too humble. What we're doing here—risking everything to save the Captain by landing on a quarantine planet with a cargo hold full of pirates—is the sort of bravery that will never be properly rewarded or recognized."

"I… I didn't know," Jack said, eyes downcast. "I'm sorry."

Mercedes sniffed, her wrath spent, and turned back to Edmond. "Do you think we'll meet him?"

Edmond didn't have to wonder who she was talking about. "I doubt we'll have a choice in the matter. He is the acting governor of Elba, after all, even if it just a false title. I suspect a ship landing on the planet isn't something that happens very often. He may take special interest."

"We must be careful, then. They say he's brilliant."

"He was a Company board member fallen from grace. The only reason he's still alive is his expert skill at Bacarrae. He bet for his freedom and won," Edmond agreed. "We must be very, very careful."

"I know it's not in your nature to suspect the worst in people, Edmond, but on Elba, you must listen to Fernand and Villefort. Their pragmatism and greed may see us through this."

"Here I thought you were going to say our love would see us through," he said, smiling.

"Be realistic. This is politics—there's no room for a bleeding heart in politics," Mercedes' voice grew sharper. At the controls, the computer sounded the warning for a successfully established orbit, and the doctor rose. "I have to get back to the Captain. We'll see you in the shuttle bay."

"I love you, no matter what happens," Edmond said. Did she know how true it was? He'd give anything to keep her safe—anything but his honor.

She smiled. "Of course I know that."

Edmond fell back into the pilot's chair, again checking the restraints on Jack. What must the boy be thinking right now? He again wondered his age, hoping he might be tried as a young offender, but the Company was ruthless when it came to pirates

"They're tight—I'm not going anywhere," the young pirate spat out, but some of the fire had left his voice. The two sat in silence as the *Dauntless* and her companion ship waited for Elba to receive them.

CHAPTER : 4

Edmond looked around the tense shuttle bay. They hadn't been permitted to land their own shuttle on the planet, but Elba was sending a shuttle to fly them straight to the Napoleon Bonaparte Clinic and Hospital. It sounded like a high-end hospital, but that only made him more worried. He'd been on enough outer planets to know the shabbier the place, the more grand-sounding the name.

Mercedes was fiddling with the Captain's med-readouts—nerves, no doubt, as he had seen her check the exact readout six times now. He had to fight down nausea every time he looked at Captain Moreau. Surely a man couldn't come back from that... could he? Still, he had survived this long.

"What's taking them so long?" the medical officer muttered, tension apparent in her forehead and the way she held her arms too close to her body.

"Typical rubes," Fernand offered from where he was lounging next to the control panel. He didn't look at her, peering instead out the transparent porthole, as if you could see something as tiny as a shuttle making the lightning-fast trip from the planet. "They like to keep you cooling your heels so you'll give them anything they ask for just to be rid

24

of the whole situation. What we should be doing is high-tailing it back to home base—not drifting into this pot of trouble."

"Has anyone told you that you mix your metaphors?" Edmond asked. He shouldn't have been so irritable, but the tension made his belly knot painfully.

"I'll mix worse than metaphors if they pull this garbage on Elba."

"Maybe you should stay here with Villefort. You could work on ship repairs while we get the Captain the help he needs. It won't take three of us."

"You need me to keep you from doing something stupid. You lead too much with your heart." He motioned to the prisoners who stood in a line in Shuttle Bay Two to be loaded onto the military shuttle that would transport them to the base prison. "Take them, for instance. We shouldn't be wasting the effort on them. Maybe, if the military shuttle hadn't arrived first, the medical one wouldn't be dragging her aft getting here."

"It would make no difference—we have two shuttle bays."

"There, you're leading with your heart, but not for your friends. Have you thought of what going planet-side on Elba might do to Mercedes' career? There's a risk that no one will take her as ship's doctor after this. She can forget sending

25

articles to prominent journals—everyone will think she has a hidden traitorous message in what she writes. She's your fiancée and you should be looking out for her, instead of these scum-of-the-earth pirates and the idiot who sailed us into this mess."

"I wouldn't speak of the Captain that way if I were you," Edmond warned. "He's a good man and worth the risk to save."

"Good man or not, we wouldn't be here if it weren't for him."

Edmond glanced at Mercedes, but she was completely absorbed in the medical readout. Did that mean she agreed with Fernand? She couldn't! Surely she wouldn't think of herself first when it came to other people's lives.

"You don't know what you're talking about, Fernand."

"I'm risking my own reputation and career to keep her safe and you out of trouble. I think that should count for something." Fernand straightened and motioned to the plexiglass that kept them separate from the open door of Shuttle Bay One. "Here comes our ride. It's too late for any more bickering. Just try to think of us when you're down there, Edmond. Not everything is a cause or a statement. Sometimes you just have to worry about yourself and your friends."

***

Medical shuttles weren't set up for sightseeing, and Fernand hogged the porthole–he hated being out of the loop–so Edmond didn't catch a glimpse of Elba until the shuttle landed on a haphazard landing pad outside the Napoleon Bonaparte Hospital.

Mercedes gave him an absentminded kiss before rushing the Captain out the door with the group of rapid-speaking white-clad personnel who had gathered to lend assistance. The medical jargon was lost on Edmond, but at least it looked like they were planning to do what they could.

He glanced around. The hospital was on the edge of the settlement—a place, he judged, of about one hundred-thousand residents. On one side of the hospital, modern city infrastructure stretched over the landscape like a mask. On the other side, the sharp, grey landscape, wreathed in perpetual mustard-colored fog stretched out. Had they factored in the creepy atmosphere when they'd designated this place a detention zone? Most likely. The Company knew just how to reduce a man to the lowest brink of sanity.

"Lieutenant Edmond Dante?" a voice called from the fog, quickly followed by a figure in military garb. "Lieutenant Fernand Mondego?"

27

"That's us," Fernand said sharply. "Who are you?"

"I'm Captain Rogers from Company Base X100B. I'm here to conduct your entry interview." Edmond nodded. This was standard protocol on a protected planet. For a moment, he thought he saw a figure standing in the fog behind the Captain. He squinted. Yes, it was definitely the figure of a short man in a billowy coat.

"I'll escort you to headquarters," Captain Rogers said with a smile. "First, Lieutenant Dante, if you would be so kind, there's someone who would like a moment of your time."

He gestured to the fog and the short man took a step forward. Edmond barely suppressed a gasp, even though he had known this meeting was inevitable. The man known in this area simply as the Governor of Elba emerged from the fog in all his disgraced glory.

He shook out his coat, letting the dust settle before saying, "Welcome to Elba. We're so pleased to provide you with the medical aid you require... and I'm sure you're ready to pay the price for our hospitality. If you've heard of me, I'm sure you've already guessed what I'll want.

"A game of Bacarrae?" Edmond asked, worried now.

The man's replying grin brightened the dull landscape.

CHAPTER : 5

Edmond was still reeling from meeting one of the most dangerous men in the galaxy when their car brought them to their destination and Captain Rogers escorted them each to an interview room.

"The interview is for your benefit. When you return, it can be used as evidence of your innocence. The Company will not be pleased that you landed on Elba—there will certainly be an investigation."

Before they were separated, Fernand gripped Edmond's elbow, pulling him in close, so their words would be for their ears alone.

"Be careful," he'd said. "What you say affects us all." His words were cautionary, but they'd hung like a threat. He had only been able to nod in response.

The interview room was sparse with only a table and indistinct soft lighting, a chair for him, and a chair for his interviewer. In a few moments, Edmond heard hushed words outside followed by a harsh, final one, and then the door opened. Nathan Napoleon, the man who'd defied the Company, stepped into the room holding a case while smiling.

"Hello, Lieutenant Dante. I thought I'd conduct your interview myself. A remarkable leader like yourself, making hard decisions like you did...

well, it's a nice change of pace. We don't get many visitors, of course, and it is always nice to speak to someone who hasn't been tainted by this place. I'd like to hear your story."

"Yes, of course," Edmond said, "but wouldn't Captain Rogers be more qualified?"

"Oh, I doubt that," Napoleon smiled, setting his case on the table in front of him and taking his seat. "Besides, I'm hoping you'll indulge a lonely man in a friendly game of Bacarrae. You play?"

Lonely? There was a whole colony here at his disposal. It was a prison colony, but still...

"I know the rules, but I wouldn't say I'm an expert. Everyone needs to know the rules—the Company sees to that," Edmond said.

"Oh, yes, the Company loves Bacarrae. You must admit it is an elegant alternative to warfare or dueling to resolve internal conflict. There is an element of chance involved. Anyone could win." He set out a board and began arranging the pieces.

"Those with the gift have a clear advantage, though," Edmond said, "and it's been said you were one of the most gifted in the company. To see another man's thoughts…" he shivered before continuing, "seems the most intimate kind of betrayal."

"Don't think of it like that," Napoleon tapped his temple. "Man has always competed with one another. Bloody acts, mostly—acts of violence. With this, however, there is no loss of life. This is classic Bacarrae, the game that started the arena spectacle we know today."

"That's one way to look at it," Edmond said, watching the man set the board with practiced ease. It had been a long time since he'd seen a physical board. Most Bacarrae matches were played out in fantastic virtual reality with incredible effects, strategies, and terrible consequences. "No Bacarrae tank here? I didn't see an immersion chamber."

"There is no need. Classical Bacarrae is by far the more elegant platform. The style means little, of course, as the game is played in here." Napoleon tapped his temple again. "We with the gift can see the surface of a man's mind—what an opponent is immediately thinking. Misleading your opponent is the other half of the game, though, both in the mind and on the board. Those without the gift can easily mislead someone with it, if they are quick and guarded."

He finished setting his pieces and Edmond began setting his in what he hoped might be a misleading configuration. He tried literally not to think about his placements, lest Napoleon read his mind. Bacarrae was a much more complex game than chess when played in board form, as well as much more exciting, even without a psychic gift to make the play double-layered.

He glanced up to Napoleon, who was watching him intently, a small smile on his otherwise blank face. "You didn't say what we were wagering, sir."

"Didn't I? Hmm," the man said, indicating Edmond should make the first move. He did so. "You landed to help your captain? Tell me about that, first."

"He and our ship were severely damaged when the pirates attacked." Edmond shrugged as he made his move. "There's not much to tell."

Napoleon made his move almost immediately, yet Edmond could tell it was decisive. "You managed to subdue those same pirates and steal their ship, instead?"

"That was Fernand Mondego's doing, our engineer. He has a devious mind." He moved another piece forward and challenged Napoleon's closest man. It turned out to be a knight, however, and Edmond's soldier was removed. "He hijacked their environmental systems and we threatened them into surrender."

"Why not just open all their airlocks?" The man's knight struck and removed another of Edmond's soldiers. "No one would judge you for killing the pirates who attacked your ship. The Company may even reward you for your heroism."

"I would judge myself," he said grimly. He smiled as he challenged Napoleon's marauding knight with one of his own, taking the other man's important piece. "Human life is important to me."

33

"Good move—and a good thought. I would ask you, though, if you know the difference between a life worth saving and one that is not." The governor's eyes turned hard and piercing; Edmond could not meet them.

"I do not care for this interview, sir, and I don't care to play a game when I haven't been told the stakes. They say Napoleon never plays a game without stakes. If you wanted a challenge, you should have interviewed Fernand, instead. He's by far the better player."

"You think so? Hmm," he moved a piece without challenging. "I'll be frank, as I see there is little intrigue about you, Lieutenant Dante. Roundabout talking does neither of us good. I see the makings of the gift in you, although it needs refining. I also see an honesty and belief in fellow man that your friends—even your fiancée—lacks."

"I didn't tell you about Mercedes," Edmond said flatly. "You're in my head."

"I told you some thoughts sit on the surface, Lieutenant. You're worried about your medical officer, and you're broadcasting that to anyone with a hint of psychic resonance. I could no more ignore your relationship with her than fail to notice your hair is black," Napoleon waved his hand, "but we digress."

When he leaned forward, Edmond did not like the look in his eye.

34

"Doubtless, when you return to your port, you will be interviewed by inspectors and inquisitors—others with the gift—who will notice you have the gift in you. You will be recruited, or coerced, into Company service. Whatever you believe about the Company is irrelevant; your skill will be their gain, and it will not be for the good of your fellow man."

Edmond tried meeting Napoleon's eye again and managed it for a moment.

"Sir, I do appreciate everything you've done—the medical attention and the promise to allow us to make repairs. You're the governor here and you could have chosen to send us away without help. This is too much, though. I've been through regulation screenings. If I had the gift, it would have been detected by now. I'm afraid you are mistaken."

Napoleon continued his hard stare for a moment longer and then relinquished. "Perhaps, perhaps. How about a simple wager? I will continue to help you and your crew, regardless of the outcome. If you win, I'll include a purse with enough to pay off your and Mercedes' debts to the Company—enough to start a new life."

"That's very... generous. If you win?"

"When you return to your port of call, look up an old friend of mine who still survives in the Company. I will give you a message for him, and he will train you without any Company biases."

35

Edmond looked at the knight he'd already managed to capture. Napoleon was a Bacarrae master. Still, put against a purse large enough to free both Mercedes and himself from their indentured service, what could one note hurt? Surely there would be no harm in that.

"You have yourself a wager."

CHAPTER : 6

The thing about Edmond Dante that was so troubling was that he didn't understand the depths of man. He was selfishly unselfish, never realizing betraying his friends to give his enemies a fair chance was the worst of disloyalty. Fernand fidgeted in his chair, letting his musings run wild as the system logged him in. It was a good thing he knew his friend's passwords—for both their sakes.

Edmond couldn't be trusted in political situations, even when he thought he should be. It was only prudent to rummage through his things to make sure he hadn't gotten himself and the rest of the crew into more trouble than they could handle. Fernand would have been more sympathetic if he hadn't seen his own chances of rising through the ranks stymied by the lieutenant's doe-eyed view of humanity and his inability to keep his cards close to his chest.

It only took a minute of quiet checking to find what he needed: notes and logs from his meeting with Napoleon. Fernand's eyes widened as he skimmed the sparse notes he had made.

"Edmond, you fool, you've doomed us all," Fernand murmured to himself. After seeing the name associated with the man's intended contact, he narrowed his eyes.

Fernand pressed his index finger to his jaw and asked, "Villefort, can you come here?"

After a moment, the doors swished open and the other man entered the Captain's office.

"Making yourself at home while the cats are away, Mondego?" he asked, placing his coffee mug down on the desk.

"That implies I'm a mouse, Villefort."

"Well, you did flee the surface and get back on the ship as quickly as humanly possible. Don't rats flee fire and flood?"

"There was no entertainment in that hellhole."

"What's Edmond been doing this whole time, then?" Villefort pulled his slate out of his breast pocket, triggered the holo feature, and twiddled with the projection so he could sort incoming messages while they spoke.

"Fussing over the Captain, flirting with our medical officer—the usual."

"Ha. Well, you weren't always so bitter about his good fortune. I always thought you were best friends."

"I was a fool. He'll ruin us. Worst of all, he probably thinks he's doing us a favor."

"Fernand, what are you talking about? You're raving a little more than usual."

Fernand pulled up the notes he'd found, along with the name of the contact, and moved so Villefort could see.

38

"He's playing Bacarrae with their little dictator."

"Sweet mother of—" Villefort jerked up from reading the notes, not quite finished.

"Yes."

"Mondego! I thought you went down to the surface to prevent something like this from happening!" Villefort's frown didn't disguise his pale face. He was just as nervous about this as Fernand.

"That wasn't up to me. We were separated for interviewing," Fernand said, crossing his arms. "It was only coincidence that I saw Napoleon leaving the room before our idiot did."

"Of course you had to break into his cabins to investigate."

"You'll be glad I did in a moment," Fernand said, leaning a little closer to Villefort with a wicked grin. "I think I finally understand the source of all your mysterious Company debt."

Furious, Villefort's face flushed, but he turned back to the notes and finished reading what Edmond had recorded. By the time he finished, his face had drained of color.

"I didn't know your father was a Napoleon sympathizer," Fernand said. "It shines a light on everything, really."

"That's what Edmond agreed to in the wager? Psychic training sessions with my father?" Villefort asked. "The interviewers will find that out—he won't be able to lie to them."

"Apparently, Napoleon thinks he has the gift. He must think Dante can get away with it," Fernand shook his head. "I rather doubt it, myself—he's never shown any kind of talent before."

"It's a shame you didn't like Elba, Fernand. Odds are we'll be back here before long as permanent residents," Villefort glowered.

"Oh, I doubt that. We'll just disappear," Fernand said. "If we do nothing, that is."

"You have a plan?"

"Of course."

"A plan to save us all?"

"Of course not, but things could work out for the two of us. We might even come out on top." Fernand cut his hand through the air with a sense of finality. "I'm through pandering to Edmond and saving him at every turn from himself. He's gone too far this time."

Villefort narrowed his eyes, but he nodded slowly. "What do you have in mind?"

"First, we must promise each other that this cannot leave this room," Fernand said. "We'll need to stand united against the investigators."

"You're planning to sacrifice your friend, Mondego. Is this something that you can do?"

"Villefort, promise me!" Fernand said. "I'll do my part."

Villefort nodded, "I swear."

CHAPTER : 7

Whatever else the planet Elba lacked in terms of luxury and freedom, the medical facilities were top notch. Mercedes had seen little else of the planet or the city; the inspector had even been accommodating enough to interview her in one of the hospital's private waiting rooms, where family waited for news of loved ones. Mercedes had had no reason to leave.

With the interview done and after a few hours of sleep, she had just replaced Edmond's vigil at the Captain's bedside and sent her fiancé off to rest. He'd looked terrible. Even worse, she had the feeling he was keeping something from her, which was very unlike him. She'd wheedle it out of him later—perhaps in bed—when they were done with this disastrous mission and back in proper civilization.

Captain Moreau was still unconscious, although his vitals had improved. Mercedes was confident that, with just a little more time, they could safely move the man back to their ship and ferry him home. Because he had been wounded in the line of work, the Company's benefit plan would surely take care of him, even though it was too early to say whether he could return to work. Mercedes drummed her fingers on her coffee cup, sipping the hot drink slowly.

Surely some benefit could be reaped from this for the rest of them, as well. Waiting had given Mercedes time to think and plan—an area in which Edmond was woefully inadequate. No matter, she had plans enough for them both, and this mission could very well accelerate their careers, despite the obvious drawbacks.

As acting captain in a time of crisis, there were sure to be accolades and bonuses awarded to him. The prize ship, while no great craft, still boasted a sound reactor and drive and could no doubt be repurposed within the fleet. Each crew member would get a purse for bringing it home.

Her quick thinking and innovation had saved the Captain's life. The company cared little for an individual life, but a captain was a valued asset and hard to replace. True, this incident may push him into retirement, or at least lighter duties, but that was hardly her fault; her skills would hopefully be recognized. An advancement in her career could mean freedom from her Company debts, and Edmond would be secure enough to propose, so they could start a proper life together, instead of sneaking around Company protocol and stealing kisses when no one was looking.

The only hitch was Elba. Their landing here would raise suspicions, and Company inspectors would ask the kinds of questions that required very careful answers. Napoleon was not to be trifled with, and the Company would think nothing of stating that saving a man's life was a poor excuse for landing on a political quarantine.

"What would you have done?" Mercedes murmured to her unconscious captain, his white hair disheveled and his normally alert eyes closed and peaceful. "We acted to save you, but perhaps you would have sacrificed yourself to save us all."

"We won't know until he wakes," came a voice from the door. It was so sudden that Mercedes nearly spilled her drink in surprise. She turned to see Fernand standing in the doorway, staring at the Captain's inert form. "It would have been more convenient for everyone if he'd been killed outright."

"Fernand!" Mercedes shook her head. "Sometimes I wonder why we're friends."

"I like to think it's because you're secretly in love with me," he said, stepping closer.

She regarded him for a few moments without speaking, but a smile played around her lips. "Don't be so sure of yourself."

"You liked me just fine in the last port." He leaned against the wall, at ease.

"Shhh. I thought you said anyone could be listening." She stood and walked over to him.

Fernand leaned in close, his words pitched for her ears only. "Would you like to be with a ship's captain someday?"

She chuckled. "Try offering me something I don't already have. Edmond will become captain from his heroics here."

"He might," Fernand shrugged, looping a finger in a strand of her hair. "Then again, you know Edmond: he might do something to jeopardize us all."

"That's quite a thing to say offhand," Mercedes said. "I thought you were back on the ship, overseeing the repairs? Do you have ears everywhere, too?"

"I have ears where they count." Fernand said. He whispered, his lips so close that she could feel them brushing her ears, "If I didn't, I wouldn't know your dear fiancé may have sunk us all."

Mercedes narrowed her eyes. "How, exactly? He has a bright future ahead of him."

"Does he? I take it he didn't tell you about his game of Bacarrae with Napoleon?"

"Bacarrae?" Mercedes's eyes widened. "What was he thinking?"

"That he's Edmond the Blessed—that butterflies and hearts come out when he exhales, and beautiful women fall at his feet."

"Fernand, this is serious!" Mercedes said. "What was the wager? What did he lose?"

"Edmond the Self-Righteous, Champion of the People." Fernand continued, "Of course he would believe he had a chance against Napoleon."

44

Mercedes grabbed the engineer by the shoulders, at last capturing his attention. "What did he lose?"

This time, Fernand leaned so close that his lips really did brush her ear in a gentle kiss. "Why don't you find out for yourself? I'd never ask you to trust me without proof."

"And if I find he's torpedoed his career?"

"Then it would be a shame for you to sink along with him."

CHAPTER : 8

The door swished open and Mercedes walked into the cabin, brushing her chin-length dark hair out of her face. With the Captain settled, sedated, and looking healthy, she should have been feeling relief. Instead, she felt like she was walking across broken glass. Every step had the possibility of either extreme pain or disaster. Did she dare hope either could be avoided?

Edmond was bent over his holo-desk, poring over reports. He worked too hard—another of his "too"s. He was too honest, too detail-oriented, and too attentive. Mercedes' mouth quirked into a gentle half-smile—it was the "too" that had drawn her to him in the first place on the Company orientation voyage. That bright-eyed, overly-perky guy on the officer track had been everywhere that first week; in the moments he wasn't around, she'd missed him so much that she'd eventually sought him out, just like she was doing now.

She leaned against the doorframe, letting her hourglass frame curve at its best angle. If the reflection in the windows was anything to judge by, her pose was just the right mix of innocence and seduction. She adjusted it by a hair before clearing her throat.

"You work too hard, Edmond."

His brown eyes were tired when he looked up, but his smile was inviting. "I'm just double-checking everything. Now that we're underway again, I want to make sure everything adds up for the Company audit. They'll go over everything we did with a fine-tooth comb."

"Stripping your work bare?" she asked while sliding a hand up her side, showing off the violin-curve of her silhouette.

"Exactly." He didn't notice her double meaning as he looked past her at the ship's crest on the wall. "I want to be sure it's all honest and above-board."

Mercedes swallowed as worry plucked at the strings of her mind. Fernand was right: Edmond was hiding something. She'd almost suspected Fernand of making it all up–it would have been very like him to suspect the worst of someone–but this anxiety wasn't normal for Edmond.

"The Captain is settled for the journey. I have a few hours before I need to check him, and you seem to have the journey in hand."

"Yes," he said absently, running a hand through his hair.

"Are you keeping something from me, my love?"

If he was, he must have known it would ruin her, too. She hadn't pulled herself up from a dirt-dweller planet-side life just to be thrust back down to it—not even for those deep, brown eyes and that charming dimple.

"Of course not," Edmond said, standing and drawing her into his arms. "Don't trouble yourself."

She felt his heart pounding against her cheek. He was concealing the truth—she knew it just by looking at him and hearing his responses. The bitterness of it made every second more precious and vibrant. His hands on the small of her back, heavy and gentle in their pressure, sent a stab of pleasure-filled pain through her.

She pulled back and took his face in two small hands. The rough stubble of his jaw made her eyes prickle with tears. If he was lying to her–and he was–this could be the last time she ever touched him like this. This could be the last time she held his chiseled jaw possessively in her hands and tasted his kiss. She indulged herself in a long, lingering taste of him. His soft lips and pliant tongue met hers in welcome, and she deepened the kiss as a pang of sorrow and desire shot from her breaking heart to deep below her belly.

His hands ran up her sides, slowly exploring, as if he hadn't done this a hundred times before. Edmond was never too anything in the bedroom—except for maybe too delicious. She met his eyes one last time, just to be sure. They were dark with desire, and his lips parted slightly. If tomorrow she chose to turn to Fernand to protect her–to keep her future from being darkened by

Edmond's–he'd see that as betrayal. He'd never forgive her.

She had to be sure.

"Tell me you wouldn't risk yourself. Tell me you're safe," she crooned, standing on tiptoes to brush her lips across his jaw. It firmed under her caress, and he took her shoulders in his hands, thrusting her back to study her face.

"You have nothing to worry about, Mercedes. I'll never hurt you—I swear." His caressing hands smoothing her hair from her face punctuated the affection in his words.

She traced his smile with her eyes. So lovely a promise shouldn't have accompanied a lie, yet it had. She closed her eyes, leaning in to kiss him again, passionate in her indecisive agony.

She had a choice now. She could sink with him, letting him believe he could protect her as they both went down in flames, or she could spare herself. She didn't like to think she was so selfish, but there was no way to save him from whatever promise he'd made if he wouldn't tell her what it was. Knowing Edmond and his chivalry, he wouldn't tell her if he thought just knowing about it could incriminate her.

With her decision made, she opened her eyes, smiling through the jagged pain in her chest. She could give him a last gift–one for herself, too– and a memory to carry beyond all of this.

She seized the front of his uniform in her fist, enjoying the surprise in his eyes, and led him toward the bed, hips swaying as she walked. He followed her eagerly, spinning her roughly as they reached the bed and scooping her off her feet to lay her gently down. Her heart fluttered with anticipation and her mouth was dry with the bitter sweetness of tasting his passion for the last time.

"I still can't believe you're mine," he said, his voice husky as he leaned over her to plant kisses from her mouth to her navel. He looked up with a flicker of a smile when he reached it. "I still can't believe you'll always be mine."

She closed her eyes so she wouldn't show the hurt in them and wrapped her legs around him as if she really wouldn't let him go. If only it were so simple—if only she could lose herself in his passion and never surface again. His kisses were fiery hot, burning a trail across her skin the way his lie had engulfed their future.

CHAPTER : 9

Edmond rubbed at his neck and shook his tired
head to try to clear his muddled thoughts.
There had been too much in the last few days
with the Captain being wounded, the argument with
Fernand about the pirates, and his game of Bacarrae
with Napoleon.

Perhaps he'd been a fool to take the wager,
but something in Napoleon's words had rung true.
He didn't have the courage to stand up to the
Company, yet, but if what Napoleon had said was
true, he already had the skills to make a difference.
This would be a new chapter in his life; if it worked
out, he would be able to provide for Mercedes
beyond what he'd been able to imagine. Very soon,
he could afford to tell her everything, but not before
she was safe. It was risky to be sure, but without
risk, there could be no reward.

"Would you have risked so much?" Edmond
murmured to the unconscious Captain Moreau lying
in the bed beside him. They were in final docking
protocols with the planet's space-side dock—a
process that could take hours—and Edmond had
stolen a few moments to sit with his mentor and
friend.

To his surprise, the Captain stirred.

"Sir?" Edmond leaned forward, searching for more signs of life. The Captain, in turn, coughed gently and opened his eyes.

"Edmond?" he rasped.

"Sir! You're awake!" Edmond said as his eyes clouded. "Even with everything we did for you, we weren't sure. The damage was extensive…"

"Water?" the Captain asked as his hand blindly searched for a glass. Edmond nodded, quickly filled a tumbler from the drawer, and put it in his hand. Captain Moreau drank, motioned for more, and drank that, as well. Something resembling his old spark shone in his eyes again, and he coughed to clear his throat before testing his voice.

"I remember pirates," he said slowly.

"Status report?"

"The ship was damaged and you were dying. We had to put into port for repairs and medical attention. Mercedes saved your life."

As he processed this, he nodded slowly. "Cargo? Crew?"

"All intact and uninjured, sir—save yourself, of course. We also managed to capture the pirate's ship when they docked with us. That was Fernand's cleverness."

"Cleverness," his mouth twitched in a sad smile, "or viciousness?"

"He did want to send them out an airlock," Lieutenant Dante admitted, "but I opted for compassion. They're in custody now, awaiting trial."

"I'd expect nothing less of you, Edmond." He passed back the cup, but before Edmond could withdraw with it, the Captain captured his hand.

"Don't lose that quality. Don't lose the compassion," he said. "There is little enough of it in this world. I should know—I've shown my share of contempt."

"Sir, I don't believe that..."

"Edmond, you've always been a great student and a better man than I was at your age. During these past years, you've taught me as much I've been able to teach you."

He settled back down into the pillows, eyes closing. "I felt it—I felt my death. There was nothing there that I'd earned in this world, except the quality of my deeds. All the regrets piled up like chains, countered only by the few acts of courage and selflessness I'd managed to accrue. I saw them all; everything was laid out plain."

"Sir, you need to rest. You've been through so much."

"Don't lose your compassion," he repeated, "it's worth more than anything else in the world." The Captain's words faded as sleep claimed him.

"I won't, sir, I promise." Edmond squeezed the man's hand and stared out the window again at the glorious planet filling his view. It was blue and green and filled with promise for those with enough courage to make their own path.

Captain Moreau's words resounded to his soul. He would meet with this man of Napoleon's and learn all he could. He would not become a tool of the Company—in fact, perhaps he could fight against it, through the proper channels, and become something of a champion. He would be a man Mercedes would deem worthy to stand by. He only needed to escape the notice of the Company a little longer before he could tell her everything.

"I will choose compassion," he whispered.

"Rest well, Captain. We're nearly home."

"Edmond, are you there?" Villefort's voice came through his comm unit.

Villefort must be overseeing the docking and investigations would soon follow. Edmond straightened his back, ready for what may come. He'd already deleted the notes he'd taken, committing them to memory in the middle of the night before purging them. There was no evidence left, save for what was in his mind, and he felt confident he could keep that safe from the inspectors and their psychic inquiries.

"Acting Captain Dante speaking," he said.

"Right, Captain Dante, the constables are here with an investigator. They want to speak to you. They're docking right now."

"They couldn't wait for the normal protocols, hmm? No matter, assemble the crew. We'll take care of this now and be finished with it."

The crew waited for him with an odd mix of expressions on their faces. Mercedes looked like glass: expressionless, but fragile. Villefort was muttering while fiddling with the holo projection from his ever-present tablet; Fernand looked, as usual, like a handsome wolf.

"Constables," Edmond said in greeting. "I think I know your intentions."

Their captain, a burly man with the signature blue half-cape and blue cap pulled tight to his ears, strode forward. "I'm sure you do. Lieutenant Edmond Dante, you are hereby placed under arrest for high treason."

EIGHTEEN YEARS LATER...

CHAPTER : 10

"Come in, Dante, and shut the door behind you," the baritone voice filled the tiny cabin of *Schrodinger's Feline*. Captain Roberts' voice always filled all available cubage, as did his ageing physique and his collection of shipyard identification plates cut from the hulls of stolen or destroyed vessels. They were arranged, with their edges warped from plasma cutters, in vertical lines on his cabin walls. There wasn't room for a single new addition.

Dante entered, limping slightly, and sat in the red leather chair facing his desk.

"I hope I'm not keeping you from party planning." Roberts' grin was decidedly shark-like. "Oh, don't play innocent. I know you're all planning a big retirement party for me. Never thought I'd leave this business, but there you have it. There comes a time when a man wants things he didn't expect, although I suppose you know that."

Dante lifted an eyebrow. He sat in the still fashion of someone highly disciplined and rigorously trained for physical action.

"You don't say much; never have since we found you begging on that wretched world. What was that place again?"

"Diappo."

"Uh huh. If Jack hadn't vouched for you, I would have left you there, but the kid's always had a sixth sense about people."

Dante stared at a place on the wall an inch above the man's head.

"Well, pirating isn't for everyone, but you've worked out. Two years and you've seen action on every station of my fine ship. You have fine instincts. It's almost like you can guess what the rest of us are thinking. You don't need me to tell you this, though." He paused, poured himself a viscous blue drink from a pressurized aluminum shaker, and swirled it in the glass. "The thing is, when you give up your ship and your crew, you want to entrust them to the right kind of person. You bought her from me fair and square with your earnings. I probably cleaned you out, too, but the thing is… well, you're so close-lipped about everything, and it would just set my mind at ease if… well. Dammit, I don't usually stumble over my words like this. Talking to you can be so single-sided, like playing zero-G ball against yourself. You could help a man out, you know."

"I'll treat the crew fairly and with loyalty."

"I never said you wouldn't. I wouldn't have agreed to sell her to you if I didn't' think you'd do right by the boys, even with all the respect you've earned. You hate the Company, too. That's always a plus."

"Yes." The single word was so solid it could have pierced a ship hull.

Roberts chuckled. "Yeah, that hasn't changed, has it? The thing is, Dante, my shuttle arrives in four hours, and it will take me down to the planet and that will be it for me. No more plundering Company ships when no one is looking. No more fat prizes and glorious assaults. I'll miss it and my crew. It would warm my bones while I play with my grandchildren if you could tell me one thing."

Dante stayed silent and still.

Roberts sighed. "Could you tell me what you're going to do with her? Raid off Asteroid Belt 007A5567? Take company purser ships near the Granadine Planets? Give an old pirate something to think of on those long, law-abiding nights."

'The *Monte Cristo.*" Dante hadn't twitched, but there was something different about the way he sat when he said it, like a man beholding beauty for the first time. His eyes glowed a little.

"A legend. No one knows where she drifted, although I grant you she's said to have a priceless treasure. The rumors fill every port. Did you catch the treasure-hunting bug? Don't go down that road—it's a fool's errand to hunt down treasure hulks. They're never what they seem."

He paused to drink, and Dante kept his steady gaze. It was unnerving, but the man was always like that: steady, deliberate, like a panther frozen in mid-leap. Roberts shivered.

In pirating, there were some crazy characters who would tell you, over breakfast, of the ghastly, horrible things they'd done. People who were clearly more nuts than the auto-doc could correct for. But at times Dante, was scarier than them all.

He was just so still and patient, like he was waiting for you to show your weakness. He'd earned it, though, hadn't he? No one knew where he'd washed up from, but he'd done everything assigned to him and done it better than anyone else could until he'd earned a big enough share to cover his take-over payment. There was no way around it, even if he was going to be a fool treasure-hunter.

"Tell me you at least have a hot tip on where to look."

"Yes," Dante said, and this time there was a hint of a smile at the corners of his mouth.

"Tell me you didn't get the tip in some space station bar. Where did you hear this rumor?"

"Chateau D'If."

Roberts snorted. "The infamous bastille where the Company kills you slowly through years of torture? Nice cover. Where did you really hear it?" He waited. "Fine, don't tell me. Not that you'll find it, but good luck to you when you give up and find something more plausible."

"Thank you for your kindness to me."

Roberts almost dropped his glass; that was the most he'd ever heard Dante say!

"Of course, yeah. I mean, it worked out, right?" he said, awkward now, before handing Dante a laser-key. "The codes and the records I bothered to keep are all on it. Treat my folks fair, be kind to the *Feline,* and I'll say nothing of your ambitions, eh?"

Dante nodded and Roberts stood to clap him on the shoulder.

"If you find the legendary bio-ship, *Monte Cristo*, then drink one in my name, alright? Watch out for aliens, too; she's not human. Now, let's go pretend to be surprised at my party."

CHAPTER : 11

Jack could feel there was something different about this day. In space, there wasn't anything as concrete as day and night, but the natural rhythms of man kept routines in place that simulated a day night cycle. So, when Jack woke for his shift and finished his morning rituals, he was not surprised to hear Captain's summons.

"We've found her," Captain Dante's voice was crisp in Jack's ear. Jack's breath caught in his throat and he sent a quick reply, hurrying through the cramped but tidy decks of *Schrodinger's Feline* with familiar ease. The ship was a little emptier than he was used to, as many of the crew had chosen to take their leave when Dante had revealed his quest, but that was fine with Jack; it meant only the faithful remained.

The bridge was typically only large enough for three to be comfortable but there were five bodies crammed into it when he arrived, some making use of video feeds from outside and others the natural windows that offered a panoramic view.

Captain Edmond Dante, a man with a thousand secrets, stood with his hands behind his back, staring out the center window. Despite the close quarters and lack of space, the other men gave him what space they could.

"There. She's been there the whole time," he said without turning around.

Quick as a weasel, Jack threaded forward to find a sliver of space between the Captain and the crew hand, Sleeveless Bill.

"You knew where to look," the young man said, shaking his head. "You knew exactly where it was. How, Captain?"

"A tip. A lot of luck," he admitted before tapping his temple. "As we came closer, it called." Jack squinted, but he'd known Edmond Dante long enough to know not to dispute anything he said. Now, the small pirate ship floated close to something straight out of legend: The *Monte Cristo*. It dwarfed their small ship the way a whale outweighed a mouse. Jack had seen dreadnaughts docked and this ship seemed as large as any of those behemoths. Its smooth lines had an organic look, like something grown instead of built. Light reflected wildly off the surface, tracing chaotic patterns against the floating rubble, debris, and ice that had hidden it for so long.

"What now, Captain?" Bill asked, breaking the silence. "She's too big to salvage and too old to fly home."

"Too old?" Captain Dante asked without humor. "Hardly."

"What will we do, then, sir?"
Dante finally turned to the men huddled around him. "We visit."

63

They flew closer, near what Jack could only assume was the bow of the great ship. He didn't see Captain Dante hail or use the communication equipment, yet a door yawned open and let them inside. It left Jack with the panicked feeling of being swallowed.

If the outside of the ship had seemed oddly constructed, the inside was outright alien. The Captain took five men with him when he strode out of *Schrodinger's Feline* and into the docking bay of the *Monte Cristo*.

Jack gaped; there was room for dozens of ships the size of their frigate to dock at once and bays to accommodate much larger ships, as well. The walls were curved with thin lines like veins evident everywhere. The faded lights inside seemed to brighten and soften with no apparent function. The ship was still powered, despite Bill's predictions, still very much alive. He shivered. They were inside a living thing, like climbing into the intestines of a huge animal. It felt wrong, even violating. What would it be like to live in a ship like this? Hopefully, he wouldn't have to find out.

"Don't stray," Dante called from far ahead. "I wouldn't use the word 'safe' when describing it." He was then off again, striding forward with the air of a man who knew exactly where he was going. The others scrambled to follow suit; Jack nearly ran to catch up.

"Captain, please, we've found it now," Jack said, jogging to keep pace. "There's something about this ship. The crew's jumpy as it is, can't you tell us what we're after? It'd go a long way toward instilling some confidence. The stories of this place... well, before today, I would have said they couldn't have been true, but now, seeing all of this, I have to wonder: is it an alien ship?"

"No person built this," Dante gestured around him.

"Does it hold infinite treasure?" Jack asked.

"Of a sort."

Jack shook his head. "I don't understand. How do you know?"

Captain Dante pursed his lips, his eyes in turmoil. "When I was in prison, I met a man who'd been here."

"What?" Jack's eyes went wide. "How is that possible? Why didn't everyone know? This ship is the discovery of the century!"

"He wasn't strong enough, he was rejected," Dante said simply, but his eyes told a deeper, more frightening tale.

He came to a large door where Veins of light from the walls converged, making it pulse. Jack took a step back when a great lid opened and a monstrous eye gazed out at them. The words came at him in his mind—soundless, yet as loud as a breaking storm. Jack fell to his knees while the others cowered. Only the Captain kept his feet.

You are the one, mind of mind, the wordless voice intoned.

"I am," Dante said levelly.

You will be tested, mind of mind, and measured, the voice continued. It sounded less like a threat than a simple fact.

"I know," Dante said.

No, mind of mind, you do not know, the voice said. *Not yet.*

"Captain, no!" Jack yelled as the pupil of the eye dilated, opening to the passage behind. Dante stepped inside as relaxed and at ease as Jack had ever seen him. The look in the older man's eyes, however, made his skin crawl.

"If I don't come out within the day, run!" he said before the eyelid closed, leaving no trace of Edmond Dante.

CHAPTER : 12

Dante's pulse raced and the blood pounded so hard in his ears that it was hard to hear anything. Around him, the walls of the passage pulsed, too. He followed the winding corridor with one hand against the wall. It neither followed a straight line, nor a curve, like you would find on many ring-shaped space stations. This corridor was organic, curving and winding with the floor rising and falling. Dante had to concentrate very hard to avoid picturing an optic nerve. The wall felt warm, but he steeled his mind, refusing to dwell on it.

This was the moment the Abbe had talked about all those long hours while guiding Dante through his mental exercises.

"You must control your own mind before you can control the mind of another," he had said. Later, he'd added, "You must learn to find the void within. Burn your emotions within the void, so others cannot use them to control you like they did when they sent you here."

Now, however, with the treasure of the *Monte Cristo* so close, it seemed almost impossible to burn the surge of excitement in the inner void he carefully maintained. Worse, his desires for revenge were bubbling to the surface.

The corridor ended abruptly and he stopped himself just before he stepped over the edge and into the cavern below. It took his eyes a moment to adjust, but when they did, he realized he was in the mouth of a huge, spherical room. The walls were lined with a patterned, iridescent blue glow like the glow some cave plants gave off. Judging by the neural shape of the patterns, though, these weren't plants. An arm–he could only think of it as an arm, despite his best efforts not to-extended from a central island, extended itself to where Dante stood, and attached its suction end with a wet sound at Dante's feet to form a bridge.

The invitation was obvious, but his stomach bucked at the thought of walking across the arm to the central hub. He swallowed hard, forcing down bile, and took a deep breath before stepping onto the arm. It gave slightly under his feet, causing a second wave of nausea to overwhelm him. He paused to let the feeling pass. The Abbe had been cagey about this part when he'd discussed his trial, and it was no wonder why.

It was hard not to stare at the patterned sphere as he walked. It was large enough to double as a cargo bay, although it was clearly not that. No, it was the mind that powered the *Monte Cristo*—that part the Abbe had been sure of. Somehow, this ship was bio-tech: living and mechanical at the same time. It had no computers, but a huge mind; no wires or circuitry, but living neural pathways running inside the walls; no regular engines or fusion reactor, but powered all the same.

"On what?" he'd asked one night in prison.

"Lost souls," the Abbe had said with a wheezing laugh.

"No, really. Tell me."

"I'm not entirely lying. It pulls dark energy from space, as best as I can tell, to fuel itself. The mind needs fuel, too, though, and for that... well, I was lucky to get away intact."

The Abbe hadn't been completely intact, although it didn't serve him well to think about such things when he was almost at the central hub. It was flat enough to stand on and about eight feet in diameter, but there were no rails, and the floor sloped in all directions. It would take nerves just to stand there, never mind the iron spine needed to be tested.

So you come, mind of mind, the *Monte Cristo* said, *and you are ready to be tested.*

"Yes." The Abbe had been very clear: any hesitance and he would be sucked dry of all neural energy in an instant.

Stand, then, with open mind, and be plumbed to your depths.

The sensation that followed was akin to the feeling of spiders running along a naked back, but internal, rather than external. Dante fed the fire within, feeding all his terror and horror into it and

69

refusing to think of what footprints this great mind might leave behind.

All creatures are fueled by desire. What you want determines what you are. What do you think the Monte Cristo *wants?*

"I don't know."

Yet, mind of mind, your want is clear: revenge.

"Yes."

You shall have it... if you pass.

"What do I need to do to pass?"

Sacrifice.

"I have nothing to give."

The sensation that followed was clearly laughter, but it scraped Dante's mind like nails on a chalkboard.

You have friends. You have a whole body, a whole mind, and a whole heart. Do you want to join with me, mind of mind, to embrace the power and wealth of the Monte Cristo? *Do you want to be one with me? To sink to the level of your species will require sacrifice from me, so I demand you make a sacrifice to prove your worth. Choose it.*

He knew he must not hesitate, yet the Abbe had said he'd failed a trial. Dante had thought he meant a rigorous mental battle. He'd prepared, training and disciplining his mind, but why had the Abbe not mentioned this? Why had he not prepared him? He had, after all, because this was the ultimate

70

challenge of the mind: knowing what you were willing to lose.

Your hesitation has cost you options. I now limit them to three. Choose between the lives of those with you, as I have no need for a crew, your memory, which is perhaps a boon after what I have seen of your thoughts, and one of your eyes, which is fitting, for I will be trapped on your plane while we are joined and shall lose much of my interdimensional sight.

He didn't dare hesitate this time. Is that what had cost the Abbe his chance?

"The eye."

After all, he only needed one for what would come next.

CHAPTER : 13

*D*ocking now.

Dante flinched as the words entered his mind with a sensation like licking a battery. The *Monte Cristo* kept promising he'd get used to it, but after so many months, the feeling was still uncomfortable.

Stop thinking about mental taste. You need to focus. This is not a pleasure journey for you and me.

The *Monte Cristo* had excellent focus. *I've set up a mask for myself so I will not draw the attention of the humans here. The uproar the mere sight of my advanced design could cause would hamper our plans. None here will know of my true self.*

Its arrogance was just as potent.

I heard that.

"I haven't been on a Company space station in years," Jack said from Dante's right. He was dressed in his best "out and about" clothing, which was a mish-mash of styles from multiple quadrants and sectors.

"You still don't want to go on leave with the rest of the crew?" Dante asked as the *Monte Cristo* slid gracefully into a notch in the space station's outer ring. Docking pins, supply hoses, and temporary passageways made their connection silently, but Dante heard their hiss in his mind as if he were the ship experiencing the sudden connection.

"I'm your man, Captain. I'll be with you." Dante nodded, schooling the pride out of his expression. It was better to be reserved in these situations. He couldn't afford to let his guard down—especially now, when he was getting so close. He and the *Monte Cristo* had planned this down to the last detail. One way or another, they would not leave this place without success. He let his mind link with the ship and his thoughts were spoken over the ship's speakers in a reasonable approximation of his own voice.

"Ship's leave granted to shifts one through three. Shift four will remain with the ship until relieved. No outsiders to be allowed aboard. All deliveries are to be approved by Captain Dante. Keenan has the watch."

"Where are we headed on-station, Captain?" Jack asked, scratching at the holo-ttoo on his neck he'd had it imprinted at the last stop. Dante was reasonably certain the cybernetic support system had a virus that was causing the itch. It made a very lifelike yellow snake as thick as Dante's arm appear to rest on Jack's shoulders, head lazily moving back and forth.

"There's a sector-wide Bacarrae tournament starting at 07:40 station time. We'll be there."

"Bacarrae?" Jack asked, following the Captain through the passage to the lift. "You don't mean the Kingmaker? The Game of Stars? The Eye-Gouger?"

"The very same." The lift deposited them outside the outer doors where crewmembers briskly headed out for a night of fun on the station. Keenan nodded his red-bearded head as they followed the stream through the anti-grav tube, grabbing the bar at the end just in time to execute the requisite flip through zero-G into the gravity of the station.

Jack gasped as they landed, feeling a moment of agoraphobia as the translucent station walls made it seem like he could reach out and touch the neighboring moons. The station outer ring encircled the dazzling light and bright fauna of the inner ring.

For New Rome Station, the Company had gone all out, recreating olive groves and vineyards between the ragged station structures. On a station like New Rome, construction was constant as one building merged into another and extra space was made for incoming people and divisions of the Company.

They landed on the dock just outside the grav tube where the light craft ferried crew members across the massive station. New Rome housed over three-hundred-thousand people and no one went anywhere on foot. Dante waved off the droid offering to drive the remaining light craft.

"Waiting for someone in particular?" Jack asked.

"The Company is sending a representative. I've led them to believe I'm Davrini Hacken."

"I guess that explains the attire," Jack said, pointing to Dante's red, hooded coat and leather pants.

Leather belts were slung across his waist, hips, and chest, as well as cinched over his thighs, and saffron lines had been brushed over his cheeks. It was a convenient ruse. The Davrini Hacken refused to associate with other societies or allow them within their territorial space; any eccentricities in his behavior could be easily explained by his origin in the famed region. On top of that, with tension high between the stoic but wealthy Davrini and the greed of the ever-expanding Company, officials at every stop from the border of Company space to New Rome Station had fallen all over themselves to make things easy for who they assumed was a very powerful man.

It has the added bonus of bringing in our old friend where you can see him. I see Henry Villefort's skimmer arriving now—convenient that he is the local liaison for Davrini Hacken.

Dante squinted into the distance for a few moments before he saw the light craft the *Monte Cristo* had already noted. It was occupied by a droid and a middle-aged man dressed in Company formal wear. He held a tablet–of course. Had Dante ever

75

seen Villefort without one? Even as his skimmer rushed toward them, his nimble fingers picked through the projected data stream, flicking data clips into new streams with the dexterity of a much younger man.

"Do me a favor," Dante said while Villefort was still out of earshot.

"Whatever you ask," Jack agreed.

"Don't speak to him."

He smiled slightly as Jack grinned. It would appeal to the young man's mischievous side to irritate a Company representative.

Don't worry. I have your psyche cloaked. Your old friends will struggle to recognize you. Plus, you took my eye. I'm sure that will help keep their memories foggy.

Don't say I've never given you anything.

The ship had been remarkably quick to pick up human humor, although ideas like civility and compassion still didn't seem to compute.
Dante fussed with his intricately-styled eyepatch as Villefort's skimmer sped the last few meters toward them.

"You should just install a holo-eye," Jack muttered, but he fell into silence as the skimmer bumped against the dock and Villefort disembarked.

"On behalf of the Company, we greet you," the man said as he stepped from the car. "I am Henry Villefort, your assigned Company representative."

76

Dante could barely keep the surprise off his face. The man was almost twenty years older—and gone to fat—but in all other respects, he was exactly the man he remembered right down to the tiny tic in the corner of his left eye. What kind of lies and swindling had he engaged in to climb so high in the Company?

Why ask when you already know the answer? We have all the details stowed handily away in my data banks...

Dante and Jack remained silent as they watched Villefort intently. He licked his lips. "With our deepest respect, we open wide our station doors in the hopes that you will find satisfaction here and consider us for future trade."

Their silence made Villefort so uncomfortable that he stowed his data pad away and ran a palm over his oily forehead.

"May I inquire which of you is the captain of this fine ship?"

"I am," Dante said.

The Company representative swept down in a low bow. "Excellent! How can New Rome help you today?"

"Bacarrae."

"The game?"

Dante stared at him as the idiocy of his question sank in. Mercifully, Jack had remained in character, silent and stern.

"   Of course," Villefort said, "of course. Come aboard my skimmer and I'll take you directly to the Bacarae tank. When did you last play?"

"Almost twenty years ago," Dante said as they clambered aboard the skimmer. Villefort waved his hand over the data stream in the control panel and they set off toward the ever-evolving skyline and deep into the heart of the spherical space station. In the center of it, the Bacarrae sphere glowed a faint aqua—whatever game was being played must have involved a water arena. When they got closer, they'd be able to see the figures moving within.

"Are you betting?" Villefort asked, stopping to clear his throat nervously. "You'll find much has changed in the past twenty years. The experience is more immersive than ever before. It's like you're right there! Observers can even choose to watch through virtual reality, as if they are in the bodies of the units being played!"

"I'm playing," Dante said.

"Oh. I really wouldn't recommend that, honored Davrini Hacken. We found monetary gains and losses were not… sufficient as motivators." Dante said nothing, and Jack, despite the twitch in his cheek of a grin trying to escape, remained equally stoic.

"So… we added physical motivations, as well. Depending on the game, you could lose a limb or be sold into servitude. There are even matches,"

Villefort lowered his voice, "to the death. We call them Bacarrae Mortalis."

My favorite kind of game.

Is that how you lost your last crew, mind of minds?

Jack forgot his promise as they skimmed closer to the Bacarrae tank and he caught his first look into the jewel-like interior. The current game looked for all the world like a war between dragons and mermaids; Jack's eyes couldn't help but follow the action as the mermaids lured the dragon into a false opening and cut him off from support to drown him beneath the waves.

"Does he really die?"

"It depends on what was bet. He's a man in a holotank, not a dragon in an ocean," Villefort said. "Not to fear! The Company regulates the betting fiercely. No man may bet what he does not have. You will not be swindled."

"If they bet his life?" Jack asked.

"He died painlessly," Villefort shrugged. "It is why I discourage visitors from betting. We are happy to trade with you; there is no need for you to play for trading routes, like our local departments, or to play Bacarrae settle your disputes. Though with you just arriving, I doubt you have disputes to settle." The Representative chuckled at his joke. Jack swallowed hard. "How did they determine their bets?"

Dante kept his eyes on Villefort. The man gave away so much more than he realized. He was a Company shill, obviously, but the way his voice shook every time he mentioned the Company told him Villefort knew his sins would one day catch up with him. He was a man just waiting for a push.

Remember what I told you: timing is everything, especially if you want this to be done with no blame attached to you.

"Easily enough. The Company has a database that lists as many variations of a bet as have been used in the past. The Company declares a bet level for each game. If you enter the game, you must choose a bet at that level or higher. If you wish to bet something that has not been bet before, the Company will evaluate your bet and determine its level. In high-level tournaments, the Company specifies the exact bet. In individual matches, the bet is determined by the challenger."

"Seems simple enough," Jack said, his eyes just a little too wide.

It was barbaric. Dante knew that and so would anyone who wasn't inextricably tied to the Company. It was yet another way for them to toy with the lives of men while making them think it was by their own free will. As always, the Company brushed a veneer of class over cruel barbarism.

That's not our fight. Pick the battles you can win and save the others until you are stronger. You're not here to kill the Company.

"Here we are," Villefort settled the skimmer in a flowering garden. Before them, pillars surrounding an entranceway rose into a Parthenon replica. "I'll take you to the game of games."

"I will go alone," Dante said.

The Company representative was nodding before he realized, and he stepped back, as if shying away from something in Dante's expression. "Of course, honored Captain. I'm at your disposal for the rest of your stay here. Please call upon me for anything you need."

"Anything?" he asked, letting the cold of vacuum seep into his tone.

Villefort nodded silently as Jack and Dante disembarked. He was still standing at the skimmer's motionless helm by the time they were halfway across the garden.

"Stop—stop and think about what you're doing. If you lose the ship, we all might as well be dragons in the ocean," Jack hissed as his superior strode toward the entrance.

"I won't bet the ship. This is a low-level match."

"If you think you're betting my life—" Dante's glittering gaze swung to Jack. He tapped his eyepatch. "Do I look like the kind of man who bets with other people's lives?"

Jack swallowed. "What are you doing here, then?"

81

Dante curled his lip in a cruel smile "Making an acquaintance with someone key to my plans."

"You're meeting a man by playing him in Bacarrae?" Jack asked, confused.

"No. I'm introducing myself by humiliating him." Dante climbed the steps of the Parthenon with a frustrated Jack at his heels. At the top of the steps was a man dressed like a Roman Centurion.

"Observation or the Pits?" he asked, thrusting his standard in their path.

"The Pits," Dante said.

"Your wager?" he asked, flicking his wrist so a holomenu fell in place where the flag for the standard should have been.

Dante placed his palm against the projection and his CV displayed, listing his false name, their ship, and the credits he had bothered claiming.

"What's on the menu for tonight?" Dante asked coolly.

"A day of servitude, five hundred credits, and the clothing you wore to the tournament."

Dante's single eyebrow rose again. "Small wagers."

The centurion shrugged. "It will be small tournaments for the next three days—base-level bets. After that, the Company games begin and the wagers will be much, much better. Would you care to choose Observation, instead?"

"Place my bet: one day of servitude."

The centurion flicked the holo, allowed it to disappear completely, and then moved the standard out of their path.

"Toss the dice and let them fall," he said, quoting the slogan of every Bacarrae tournament on a hundred worlds.

"Does that mean 'good luck?'" Jack asked.

"In a manner of speaking," Dante said.

CHAPTER : 14

Dante settled into the small, comfortable command chair and leaned forward at the beckon of the pretty attendant so she could attach the crown.

"Is this your first time?" she asked, making small talk as she adjusted the golden ring to fit snugly over his temples. "I don't mean to pry, but you don't have any feedback scars."

Dante smiled at her. "I've played," he gestured vaguely at the command pod and the massive globe in front of him, "but not like this." "Oh! Well allow me to say, please enjoy your very first game," the girl said before giggling. "Your accent is wonderful. Where is it from?"

"Davrini Hacken," Dante said, touching the crown on his head. He was already feeling the connection to the system, even though he didn't need it—through the ship, he could interface with a staggering array of psychic technology as easily as breathing. He was still getting used to the sensations, but he was learning so much.

"Oh? Oh!" The girl nearly input an incorrect setting as she realized the importance of the man sitting in front of her.

Dante gave her a disarming smile. "Not to worry. I am just a man making a bet."

The attendant nodded but remained tense. "The game will begin in a moment, sir," she said, bobbing her head. "Please use the ordering service if you need anything. Any taste or appetite can be accommodated on New Rome." She stressed before leaving. When the door closed, Dante settled into the chair. He didn't need to close his eyes, but he did so, anyway, as he let the connection to the game come fully online.

His was presented with a loading screen where he needed to set his preferences—this was his first Bacarrae match on New Rome and the system didn't know him yet. He entered his critical information and locked it in, attaching his bank account. Next, he was presented with a dizzying array of different commander avatars to assume in the game. Each commander had a diverse selection of units that would be available for selection in the match. There were limits as to how many units each commander could bring to field, and the game computer kept the sides fair. Every unit had its own strengths and weaknesses, as well as some special abilities. Every commander avatar had a single-use, powerful special ability. All in all, there were many strategic options to consider. A high lord elf commander in golden armor caught his eye, and he smiled while reading briefly through that commander's specifics. In Bacarrae, the commander was everything—lose that unit and you lost the game. While playing, Dante could take direct control of any of his units.

I like the giant floating brain.

You would. I'm choosing the elf lord—I like the crown.

You would.

Dante finished configuring his profile and locked in his choice. He was immediately transported to the negotiation space. He faced four others, each an avatar of the army he would face, except for the official who would oversee the game. As always, the official appeared as a helmed knight with his or her face obscured. The others were an angel with one black wing and one white wing, a gleaming humanoid robot, and an elemental that looked to be made from raging storm clouds. Dante, himself, appeared as the high elf with a tall crown and a long, sharp sword.

"The rules of this low-level game dictate restricted use of special abilities. Players, the wager stands at clothes, a day of servitude, or five hundred credits. Base-level bets as allowed by Company code THZ-0015," the official said. "Do all agree?" The elemental scoffed, "Paltry sums—hardly worth the effort."

"Do all agree?" the official asked again.

" Yes," Dante said, bowing a little. "Luck to you all."

"Luck will have nothing to do with it when I steal the clothes from your back," the elemental said with a laugh. "We agree." The others nodded.

"Very well. Fourth seat has choice of arena," the official nodded to Dante.

"Woodland hills."

"Typical elf player choice," the robot said.

"The board will be set and the winnings will be collected when the victor is determined." The official nodded again, and Dante found himself back in the command pod. He sighed and reached out with his mind, quietly touching each of his opponents. He knew they would be doing the same to determine his strategy and gain insight into his weaknesses. He drew on the power of the *Monte Cristo,* and he and the great mind effortlessly put together a false front. He felt it being probed, but not shaken, by the other players and he smiled. He turned his mind to his opponents.

This might be amusing.

The elemental was an arrogant young man full of bravado and raw skill. He would be playing aggressively, hoping to quickly hamstring one of the others and take them from the match. The robot was slower, more thoughtful, and would rely on defense. The angel was the strongest of the three, Dante determined, and had enough control of his thoughts that he wouldn't be able to penetrate without revealing his strength. He abandoned the probe as

87

the players chose and set their game units; he had that chore to tend as well.

The walls of the command pod disappeared and he was floating in midair. Around him, in the Bacarrae arena, a vast forest started to grow into a tangle of brush and tall trees that would be perfect for his elves to wage their war.

They'll never see me coming, Dante thought, satisfied.

Careful, you've not won yet.

He quickly arranged his units and the game began.

He moved to meet the elemental army first, his elf units rushing through the forest unencumbered by the tangled brush. He quickly discerned the elemental player's strategy, reading his mind with deft touches of mental prowess while revealing a false plan to the smug man. When the elemental player expected to be rushing a hidden troupe of elven archers, he found instead an elven magic user protected by knights with strong shields. Howling with wind and empty bluster, the elementals fell quickly as the wind and lightning broke upon a shield wall.

The angel had begun probing the robot's defenses, and explosions from robotic guns met bolts of light from the angels. The player's commander was revealed: a massive archangel holding two gigantic swords with one black wing and one white wing. In the player's mind, Dante saw an angelic assassin moving silently toward the robotic leader under an angelic illusion spell. While the other player was occupied with the front lines, the angel performed regicide to remove the robot from play.

"Seat two has lost." The official appeared over the arena and pointed his sword at the robot player's side of the board. All his units faded from existence.

"Then there were three," Dante murmured, impressed at the commander of the angels, who now rallied his troops again, this time against Dante. Dante found himself facing the remains of two armies at the same time. He faded his units back a little, laid his trap, and waited.

The elementals rushed in, of course. The remaining units backed up by the storm cloud elemental commander converged on a unit Dante projected as his commander, but was really a normal soldier. The soldier was sacrificed but the elemental units perished in a rain of arrows from hidden archers. Elf knights with their tall shields moved to block off their commander's retreat. The fight was fast and furious, but in the end the elemental commander fell without support from his other units. The howl of rage from the young man echoed in his mind, and Dante felt him throw the crown from his head in disgust. He turned his full attention to the remaining angel player.

He reached out, scanning the man's mind for an advantage. The surface was mostly blank, save for a few fleeting thoughts kept under tight control. Dante looked past those false fronts and felt the resistance of the other man, futile though it was. A little more pressure and he could see everything. In a moment, he saw the player's plan and layout of his units and immediately left the other man's mind. A thin smile graced Dante's lips as he moved in for the kill.

Is he the one? He sent the thought to the *Monte Cristo* in orbit.

Yes. This is Albert, son of your enemy Fernand Mondego.

CHAPTER : 15

Where had this Bacarrae been eighteen years ago when he was a younger man? This was far beyond any of the games he'd experienced before. Dante wove in and out of the perspectives of his elven army with a rush of excitement. Was there anything better than taking a chance and matching your skill against the skill of another? This game felt as real as if he was, in fact, a wood elf running alongside his units as they charged up a sparsely treed butte.

The angel army chased after them, never realizing Dante was projecting a false image on their leader's mind. While it looked like his entire force was congregating on top of the butte, it was only one of his remaining units; the rest were hidden in the sides of the bowl-like valley below, waiting for the last of the angel army to enter it. There would be nowhere to run.

He kept half an eye on the battle, but his mind was occupied with trying to slip behind the young man's mental shield. It was cleverly wrought, and the boy's mind was sharp and quick. Surprisingly, he was nothing like his father. Where Fernand had been crafty and impulsive, the boy was iron-willed and deliberate. Perhaps he'd inherited those traits from his mother.

A blur of movement to his right was all the warning he had, but it was enough. He ducked to the side, mentally commanding two of his nearby knights to attack. The elf to his left slashed at the angel unit, but his sword passed right through it. An illusion! The real threat was a black-skinned angel assassin that appeared out of nowhere, hidden by one of the angel unit's abilities. The boy had almost caught him off guard—he was talented, indeed. Would that be a problem or a boon with what was to come? Only time would tell.

Dante smiled. The boy was clever, but it would not be enough. Finally, he revealed his commander: the high elf lord stalked forward with sword held in low guard. The elf lord was a force of nature under his superb mental command. Whirling steel countered every strike as Dante felt every attack coming before it was made. High elves sprang from their hiding spots, rushing down the valley and finishing the Mondego boy's pinned forces. As the last angel unit fell, Albert's commander appeared in front of Dante's avatar in a frantic, last ditch attempt at victory with both massive swords held high. Oh, he was a tricky one.

Dante finished him with a sudden strike even as he danced around the heavy swords of the angel commander.

"Seat three has lost. The game is awarded to seat four. Penalties to be determined by the winner." The official droned as the game arena faded away. His

92

own army vanished and the other three avatars appeared before him in the negotiation space, along with the helmed moderator.

"You'll pay for this," the leader of the elementals said. "These level-zero games are just playing around. If you stay for the big leagues, I'll remember your name and take everything you have. I'm with the Red League, and the enemy of one is the enemy of all."

"You can try." Dante kept the frown off his face, but this was bad luck. He hadn't meant to make more enemies before he dealt with the ones he already had, and if he didn't rise high enough to play in the higher-tier games, all of this would be for nothing. Still, it didn't do to show weakness to snot-nosed kids, whether they were well-connected or not.

"Is that some kind of threat?" the elemental player almost spat, despite being an avatar.

"No threat. Only facts."

The sound of sheet metal tearing filled Dante's ears and then the elemental player's voice abruptly stopped.

"Communications privileges have been removed from seat one," the administrator said. "Seat four will now state the penalty he will take from the losing players."

"I'll take the money," Dante said. He would have liked to see the elemental run home naked, but he needed the credits, even sums as small as these.

"Fees have been deducted from the losing accounts and credited to the winner. Rank changes based on today's scores, times, and bonus elements have been combined with the average of your ranking for the past thirty days and added to the leaderboards. Congratulations."

The game faded from Dante's consciousness and he found the attendant removing the golden ring from around his head. His ranking was displayed on the wall behind her: *Captain of the Monte Cristo: 4,356.* He scanned the wall until he saw *Albert Mondego of Mondego Industries: 2,763.*

"Can I request seat three for a drink?" Dante asked the girl.

She laughed. "Are you a mutual admiration club? He just sent you the same message."
On the wall under their scores, a message floated. *Please allow me to express my admiration in the form of drinks on the observation deck.*

Dante's heartrate sped. He'd been waiting for this moment—or one like it—for so long that it almost felt unreal. His palms sweated as he stood and composed himself. He'd have to play it just right; he couldn't afford to tip his hand. Albert Mondego would need to believe Dante was his ally and nothing more.

He swallowed and headed for the most important meeting he'd had in eighteen years.

94

CHAPTER : 16

Dante wasn't sure what to expect when he met with Albert , but Jack insisted he be careful.

"Who is he that he's so important? Other than dangerous, of course," he asked as the two walked side by side toward the observatory lounge.

The screens that hovered all around showed the current game in progress, along with several others, as the preliminary skirmishes were fought by lightweights and wannnabes—precursors for the world-altering event that would begin in a few days.

"He is important to my plans," Dante said. "He may be my way into the main tournament." Jack almost stopped. "You plan to enter?"

Dante smiled. "I plan to win."

"I watched you play. I don't know the game, but it's obvious you do. The player running his mouth could be trouble. This game is dangerous, Captain. It has ruined men."

Dante nodded. "It will ruin many more." He stopped short of the lounge door and grasped Jack's shoulder. "Trust me. This will make all our fortunes."

The young man stiffened and then nodded. "You know we're with you, Captain. Every one of us owes you his life and more. Now, with the ship—"

"The ship's worth the cost. There, he's waiting for me. Wait close by and watch the door. I won't be long."

Worth the cost? I'm worth so much more than that.

Dante took a breath and steeled his mind. He'd never seen the dark-haired boy sitting at the lounge before, but he knew him. A mind was a unique thing—an elegant construct vastly more complex than a fingerprint. Having taken the measure of the man's thoughts during the game, he could sense him now. His features shocked him, though. His eyes and the smile he flashed as Dante approached made him sure this was the son of Mercedes. The resemblance shocked him more than he'd expected. His schooled mind remained in control, but just barely.

This is the man. He is your enemy?

I don't know, yet. This seemed to satisfy the Great Mind in the ship.

"Captain Monte Cristo, I assume?" Albert stood and smiled warmly, extending his hand. "Well played! That was amazing! I can't believe how good you are at this—but you're from Davrini Hacken, aren't you? Do you play there? Having front row seats to that performance was well worth the cost of losing."

"You have me at an advantage," Dante said, returning the smile, even though he had to steel his heart. The mouth and the dancing fire in his eyes were Mercedes', obviously. All these years later, her betrayal still pained him.

"I had to ask the attendant and perhaps promise her a rendezvous later to learn your name. The lists are confidential, of course," Albert said before bowing low. "I am Albert Mondego, son of the famed Fernand Mondego and an officer of Mondego Industries, an authorized division of the Company. I am pleased to make your acquaintance." He looked too young to be half of all that and his boyish features were alight with enthusiasm.

"As am I," Dante said, nodding, "but why single me out like this?"

Albert indicated the chair next to him at the bar. "As you well know, Bacarrae is as much a game played outside the arena as it is inside—it pays to have strong allies. We could do this together, Captain. I'm in need of a good ally. My father... well, I need to prove I'm up to the task of playing in these games on behalf of Mondego Industries."

"Ah, politics," Dante said, taking the seat and motioning to the bartender for a drink. "I meant to meet with you, as well, for similar reasons. I'm new to New Rome. You play very well."

"All the more reason to strike an alliance— at least until the finals," Albert said. "You'll be entering the tournament?"

"It's the reason I came," Dante smiled. "There is much to gain here."

97

"You've got that right," Albert laughed, taking a sip of his drink. "You've already made an enemy, though, or so it would seem."

He tipped his head to the right, indicating a booth where three men muttered amongst themselves. They were well-dressed men of popular fashion and influence. A man with long, blonde hair looked in a particularly foul mood as he scowled into his drink and turned bitter glances toward Albert and Dante at the bar.

"That was the mouthpiece you beat first in the game, Richard Costel," Albert said. "His father owns hotels and bought his position on the Red League, but he's starting to earn his own way. He's a nasty piece of business with a hot temper."

"A worthy opponent?" Dante reached out with his mind and felt for the other man, where he found pettiness and anger before receding.

Albert shrugged. "Perhaps. I have my own friends and, of course, my father is a notable Bacarrae player with a reputation for ruthlessness. I'm not scared of Costel. In my experience, good men draw the ire of the weak."

Dante took a slow drink while his mind raced. He steeled himself for what he needed to do. "You presume much without knowing me."

"A calculated risk—I'm willing to take the time to find you out," Albert said. He stuck out his hand. "What do you say to an alliance in these games?"

98

Dante looked at his hand for a moment and then took it. "Toss the dice and let them fall."

CHAPTER : 17

"**Y**our friend's a real talent," the man beside Jack said as they watched the glowing sphere from outside. "I haven't seen a string of wins like this in a very long time."

The observation decks were open to any comers, but virtual tickets were sold for the better seats. From anywhere in Observation, you could view the arena through a virtual lens and see whatever you wanted, including riding in one of the units' heads and pretending you were a player. Somehow, none of it beat watching it live with your own eyes. Dante had paid for tickets for Jack on the reserved level for every game. He had a bird's-eye view, and moveable portions of the deck could be navigated around the outer shell of the sphere to watch from any angle he chose. If he was just here for fun, it would be the experience of a lifetime—although he'd had several of those since meeting Dante.

"Almost as good as the legendary Napoleon. I saw him play once before he was exiled to Elba."

"Really? How did you manage that?" Jack asked. He felt strange in the tailored, high-end clothing Dante had bought for him after his second win. "We must look the part," Dante had said, but it still felt strange to wear clothing that pretended he was something other than what he was. It did give him an advantage with a better class of people, however; women who usually ignored him allowed him to buy their drinks and remarked almost favorably on his holo-ttoo.

"I'm a reporter," the man said. "I write for the Interstellar Times."

He flashed a grin that showed perfect white teeth, and now that Jack looked, he saw his face had been biosculpted to near-perfection. Jack had never liked that look—it was like one of his sisters' dolls had come to life. He smiled back, but the man gave him the creeps.

"I missed his first game because I wasn't watching for him. Who would have thought a Davrini Hacken would arrive and then play a *minor* game? But that's his charm, see? Mysterious, foreign, and an underdog.The story sells itself."

"Does it?" Jack asked, signaling the waiter drone. It slipped over, dispersing drinks and smiling in a charming fashion. Whoever had decided serving drones should look like bombshells had either been very thoughtful or extremely cruel. You could never strike out with them, but what would be the point?

"Of course it does," the reporter said, holding a foppish viewmaster up to his eye for magnification, as if the dome surface wouldn't magnify for you if you asked it to. "I saw his second game with Albert Mondego, the Mondego heir. He's a clever choice of ally. The Mondegos are a force to be reckoned with. They were overwhelmed by six opponents.I thought for sure they would lose—and with what Mondego bet, his family would have lost three quarters' profits—but no, your friend swooped in and turned the tables!" He gave a low whistle. "Now *that* reminded me of old Nathan Napoleon. He didn't work for him, did he?"

Jack ignored the serpentine gleam in the other's eye. "Of course not."

The reporter shrugged. "Worth asking. Did you?"

Jack raised an eyebrow.

The reporter held up his hands. "Don't be upset. I have to ask—it's my professional obligation. I did notice you bet heavily on him on top of the bets he placed, himself. Between the two of you, there must be a fortune won already."

"It's not illegal," Jack said.

"I never said it was, although I've heard rumors that the Company is watching you. I even heard rumors that they were funding the Red League's vendetta against your friend. Do you know anything about that?"

Jack shrugged uncomfortably. Could it be true? If it was, then they were making bigger enemies than they knew.

"That third game—whew! What a clincher! He and Mondego split forces to make that pincher move, but they were out of the minors by then and into standard games. Being foreigners, I doubt you know what happened to Kelliher,the man who tried to flank him. It wasn't pretty, I can tell you."

102

"Fired?"

His eyes widened. "You didn't hear? His employer removed his right hand and sent him to the fringe colonies as a moisture farmer. These games aren't a joke, you know."

Jack swallowed. Fancy suits, bubbly drinks, and not a law broken, yet these civilized people were more brutal than any of the pirates he'd served with.

"Now here they are in the advanced games. They are quite the crowd favorites. See them cheering on the free deck?"

Below them, a crowd of young people painted with the white and black angel wings of Albert and the now-infamous golden diadem of Dante's avatar performed a choreographed dance together, swords flashing gracefully and deadly.

"I'm surprised they've provoked the Red League, even not knowing they were Company-backed. The next game will determine whether they can compete in the great games, and if they win this one, they will be playing almost entirely against members of the Red League."

Jack was silent as he stared at the game. With an assassin-quick strike, Dante made the pivotal move that was sure to win him the game. Jack nodded companionably to the reporter and made his way to the lower levels. He'd meet Dante when he came out, as always. The man was far too blithe about his physical safety; Jack, on the other hand, trusted no one.

He turned a corner just before the doors and was hit hard in the jaw. What the-? He stumbled to the side, as the "reporter" raised a stun bar for the second time.

"The Red League has many friends," he said, "and so does the Company."

Jack flipped to the left, spinning around the man's flank and delivering an expert roundhouse kick to the back of his skull. He spun as he fell, and Jack snatched the bar from his limp hand. He dropped to the ground, placing a knee precisely on the man's sternum and exercising just the right degree of pressure.

"So does the Captain. Next time, don't bring a stun bar."

"Why not?" the man gasped.

"Because it hurts when your own weapon is turned on you."

He zapped the man in the center of his chest, letting his body buck and twitch before throwing the bar aside and striding away. He'd recover, but he wouldn't forget a lesson like that.

Dante needed to make his move soon. He was acquiring too many enemies.

CHAPTER : 18

Villefort dropped Dante off in the skimmer. "As always, I wish to express that we are so grateful to you for accepting our hospitality."

Dante didn't listen, his mind on the game ahead. It was a level-four bet, and if he lost this one, he would suffer grievous harm to either his person or his credit account.

"I thought you could, perhaps, use some personal attention from me." Villefort's eye tic was more pronounced as he spoke. "The Company requires certain protocols for the profit from bets. I could help you keep your dealings legal with no extra charge—as a friend."

"How would that work?"

"If you gave over signing authorization for you, I'd deal with all your legal work. You could forgo the standard skim the Company takes on your profits and I will find you better rates."

"I'll think on it."

Villefort's smile was a bit too eager. Ah. So that was his angle. He was either planning to skim some off the top using his "signing authority" or frame Dante in Company tax evasion by not paying the rates correctly. He and the *Monte Cristo* had wondered exactly how Villefort had gained access to so many foreign accounts. Now they knew.

Oh, he does more than that. I've been watching. Money laundering through multiple accounts, loan sharking, and a lot of skimming— he's a busy man.

He won't frame me again.

No. This time, we'll be working an angle.

Dante entered the Bacarrae rooms, his mind occupied with Villefort, and sat in a now-familiar command chair.

This will be the hardest fight thus far, he told the ship.

It is inconsequential. You will not be overcome by the minds of the men before you.

Even so.

You are frightened, mind of mind? Let me burn that from you. There is no room for fear for what you plan to do—for what I have planned for you.

I will not allow you to take my humanity.

Fear is what keeps me human.

What is humanity? Weakness bundled in frail flesh? I offer transcendence. Release. Freedom.

I will finish the work I've started and I will finish it as a human.

This is your decision. You have my assistance, as we agreed. Take of my strength, as you require it.

Dante sent nonverbal thanks and pulled his mind back to the present, opening his eyes. The same attendant from his first match was there with the crown. She waited patiently while he finished his commune; she must have suspected he was involved in some sort of pregame ritual. A smile tugged his lips at what she might think of him if she knew the truth.

"I'm sorry, I haven't asked your name," Dante said, bending his head to accept the crown. "You've been assigned to me?"

"Lily, sir," the girl said as she adjusted the device and powered it on. "Truth be told, the other girls are too frightened of you."

He let out a small bark of a laugh. "Of me?"

"Well, of a Davrini Hacken," Lily said, turning her gaze down. "Since I served you first, without knowing, I know that's not true. You're not dangerous—at least, not to anyone outside the arena."

"I'm notorious?" he asked. Without having to look deeply into her, he knew the girl had no ill will against him. "Thank you for taking care of me and keeping me from enemy sabotage."

Lily stuck out her lip a little, fire in her eye. "Not while I'm setting the controls, sir," she stated plainly. "Whatever happens to you will be your own doing."

"I believe you," Dante said, inclining his head and then settling into the chair, ready for the match ahead. "You will be rewarded for your troubles."

He let his mind slip, and soon he was in the negotiation field with his companion, Albert.

"They're out for blood, Captain," Albert said over a private channel. "We'll need to be careful—I doubt any part of this match will be fair."

"We're more the match for them," Dante said, sizing up his opponents. Among them was Richard's elemental leader. "They won't see what's coming."

"Do you know something I don't?" Albert asked, eagerness filling his voice.

"If you only knew..." Dante said before turning his attention to the official.

"This is a gateway match. Any participants who succeed here will earn both the rewards of the bets, as well as entry into the grand battles of the tournament," the official said, pointing his helmed gaze at each player. "Your bets have been placed and the pot stands at a half million credits. To the victor go the spoils. The arena has been randomly chosen, so no clear advantage can be garnered. It will be the Forbidden City. Luck to you all."

"   Forbidden City?" Albert said over the private channel. "Red must have paid a pretty penny to have that chosen. The arena clearly favors three of the four opposing sides and neither of us!"

"It won't matter," Dante said, focusing his mind on his opponents. "Here they come."

The match should have been three teams of two against each other, but the Red Legion clearly had other plans, and there were no rules against four players teaming up against two, nor even five on one. Ruthlessness was a praised attribute of a Bacarrae player. Dante sensed that all four players were coming at Albert and himself in a rush; they wouldn't have long to make their moves.

He issued his orders and fled his body, taking direct control of his elven king avatar. With a battle cry that was sure to raise cheers from the audience, he summoned a griffon and jumped astride it, commanding the beast to make its way to the top of the nearest tall building. There he sat tall, a target for any of his rivals.

The ancient city stretched out ahead of him, the stone work a maze that could easily be used to anyone's advantage, if they chose. Dante moved the griffon two steps to the left just in time to miss being struck by a bomb launched from a dwarven war machine. He smiled as he marked the location and commanded his hidden archers to launch a volley in the same direction. He then drew his sword, held it high, and launched himself into the maze of buildings.

He'd announced his presence and location to his attackers and sent an aggravating assault. As he felt out the thoughts of those racing toward them, he smiled. Their anger was obvious and their intentions ignoble. No matter, he knew the location of every unit and how best to defeat them. Their minds were open to him.

Dante urged the griffon down what might have been a blind alley. A dwarf miner popped out of the ground just in front of him, and he swung his sword the moment its head cleared the earth, dispatching it easily. A band of green-skinned goblins in fearsome red war paint launched themselves from the tops of the surrounding buildings and fell with knives outstretched. As they fell, Dante's sword cut two of them clean in half, and he spun the griffon in a circle, its wings sweeping the others from the air and smashing them heavily into the wall with minimal damage to himself. The griffon's sharp talons made short work of the stunned units, and Dante plunged toward the end of the alley.

"They call you the Captain. Captain of what, I wonder?" a voice sneered in Dante's ear. He wheeled the griffon around at the of the alley to face Richard's avatar, the swirling mass of power at the head of elementals, dwarven warriors, goblin marauders, and slavering beast men.

"Captain of Defeat? Captain of Despair?" Richard sneered.

"Maybe so," he pointed his sword at his enemieswith a snarl., "but you're going to have to come here to find out."

The elemental made a howl like a storm and led the charge.

CHAPTER : 19

A horde of creatures swarmed into the alley bolts of power and arrows as their vanguard. Richard and his cohorts seemed less concerned about losing units of their armies to friendly fire and more in ending Dante. Goblins in flying machines swooped from above alongside hawk men with savage stone hatchets, cutting off escape from above. The elven king sat astride his great mount and watched them come. At the last instant, he sheathed his sword, bowed his head, and disappeared.

"I told you it would work," Dante said on the private channel to Albert, where his avatar was positioned high above the alley. Three angel magic users cast spells beside him, finishing the ability that had kept the illusion in place to trick the oncoming army. It was same trick that had almost ended Dante in their first match, but it was assisted by his psychic interference this time.

"I still don't know how..." Albert's angel shook his head. "They have magic users and almost one hundred eyes—someone must have spotted the illusion and figured it out—but I suppose that doesn't matter now." He lifted his sword and pointed it at the alley overrun with enemies. "Fire."

Dante sent his command in a less verbal form, but it was nevertheless just as effective. Elven archers sent volley after volley of arrows into the alley. Angels added heavenly fire, and Albert used his commander's special ability to summon a massive solar flare that pierced the clouds and struck the alley, devastating it and slaying many of the lesser units outright. Dante smiled when the score board showed two of their opponents had been executed. He noted, however, that Richard still needed to be dealt with—something that deserved to be attended to personally, Dante decided. His griffon swept down to the battlefield with long, steady strokes of its wings.

Elven warriors went before Dante, along with Albert's angels. His mind went out before him as a scout, sensing each player's mind, penetrating their weak defenses, and determining the placement of every danger. The Red League would have no chance to walk away from this engagement, but that was hardly his fault. He hadn't sought them out as enemies, after all, and they were merely a stepping stone toward his goal—as was Albert, he admitted to himself.

A goblin hunting party was cut down before they had a chance to surprise anyone. Arrows were sent toward dwarf miner locations before their heads even broke the surface of the arena. Beast units with their camouflage ability activated were no more hidden to Dante than if they'd stood in plain sight. The only type of unit he didn't encounter was elementals. Richard was up to something.

"Be careful—he'll be using his special ability somewhere," Albert said over the private channel.

"It's too bad you've already used yours," Dante said back.

"You summoned that griffon as your first action!" the young man retorted. "You're hardly in a position to lecture me."

"The griffon was important to the plan," Dante said. "I don't have wings strapped to my back."

"Hmph," Albert said. "Just be on the lookout. 'Combine' is a very powerful ability, and Richard might be desperate, as he stands to lose a lot in this match. It will ruin him."

Ahead of them, a thunderhead was forming, funnel clouds reaching out to lick at buildings and streaks of lightning lancing down to strike. In the eye of the maelstrom, Dante knew Richard's avatar was summoning his special ability. All of the other elemental units retreated toward the storm and Richard absorbed them, one at a time, growing strong and bigger in size.

"At least the ability is obvious."

"And you joke," Albert said, his avatar shaking his head, wide-eyed. "I hope you have a plan for how to deal with that thing."

Dante grinned. "With style. Follow me in and watch out for lightning."

The Captain of the *Monte Cristo* dove and wove a complex flight path through all the arrows, fire, and bombs the enemy could muster—far less than when they'd first engaged. He sent small bands of elf warriors to harry the larger, slower units in the beast men army, hitting targets of opportunity before fading away. Even with all his foresight, he lost some units. He concentrated most of his attention on the elemental avatar, growing as large as a skyscraper in front of him as it consumed the rest of the elemental army into one unit. It was typical to put all hope into one overly large unit. Still, it was a target his archers could hardly miss.

Elven archers fired and angels added their heavenly fire, but the massive elemental unit took only small amounts of damage.

"Too bad I wasted my special," Albert commented. "It might have been enough to at least wound him."

"If you hadn't, he would have combined with even more units and would be even harder to stop now," Dante said. "You made the right choice. Now we just need to slay a giant."

"I still don't see how."

"Do you see that old tower?" Dante asked, sending the exact picture of the building through the system. He then sent a quick simulation of his intentions.

"You're mad!" Albert exclaimed. "The timing alone... and he needs to be in the perfect position!"

"Let me worry about positioning. You be ready to do your part."

Albert was silent for a moment, but then he sent his agreement. Dante turned his griffon away and down, toward the monstrous storm elemental and what looked like certain doom. Stray arrows flew against him, but he dodged them easily or swiped them from the air with his sword before they could cause any harm. Below, he sent his elf warriors on a mission to ferret out what enemies they could, until the giant elemental turned his storm against them and either destroyed the smaller units outright or sent them scurrying for cover. Dante ground his teeth as he watched his units decrease. He was risking much—everything, in fact—on this play.

Swooping in close to Richard's avatar, he narrowly missed being swatted from the sky by a giant hand before swerving hard to miss the lightning blasts that followed. Even though it was a simulation, Dante could have sworn he smelled ozone from the closeness of the strikes. As he wheeled around, he sent out probing thoughts and sought out Richard. With the help of the great mind, he easily saw his opponent's intentions and began to subtly influence them. Like a master playing a violin, Dante changed Richard's thoughts and brought the man's anger to the forefront.

"   Do you see?" Richard called over the general channels as his huge avatar plunged through the city after the elf king, sending blast after blast of lightning at his smaller foe. "There's nowhere to run! No matter what happens, Captain, you will lose!"

"I think not," Dante sent back, carefully watching the charging unit behind him. The timing, as Albert had observed, had to be perfect. He was aware that his ally had brought his own avatar into place, not trusting his lesser units with this all-important task. Lightning burned feathers, it struck so close, and Dante had to struggle to keep control of his mount as he climbed up and away, higher and higher. The positioning was almost right...

"Now!" He turned his griffon around and brought it into a screaming dive directly at the elemental's head. Wind brought tears to his eyes, despite the simulation, and he held his sword out. At the same instant, Albert's avatar sent a withering blast of holy fire not at the elemental, but at the base of the tower directly behind it. The base weakened and started to fall, it's sharp tip coming into line with the elemental's heart with each fraction of a second. Dante, smiled as he lashed out and swooped away, not causing much damage, but making the elemental stumble backward from the force of the attack. It fell into the spear of the falling tower, old masonry

116

punching through the heart of the storm and causing a huge explosion that lashed out and destroyed everything it touched. Dante winged away just in time, whooping.

One by one, the other players singled their defeat and resigned from the match. Richard, before he signed off, sent one last message. "You still lose, Captain. It didn't matter. You still lose."

Dante suddenly had a sinking feeling and reached his psychic self toward Richard, pushing past the man's mental defenses. He felt the fear of the man and swept away his weak defense. Below the surface, Dante plumbed deeper to find the plot laid out plain: the Red League had hired men to kill him and Albert.

Dante's pod door opened and two men rushed in with knives. Jack appeared from nowhere and clubbed the first one from behind, sending him bouncing off the nearby wall before grabbing him and throwing him from the room. Dante moved to dodge the low thrust of the second man, but got caught in the cables of the crown. He'd brought his arm up too slowly to block the blade completely, and as pain lanced through his forearm where the blade bit, he flinched away.

Not this human.

Dante felt the great mind of the *Monte Cristo* in a way he hadn't before. It was a physical presence—a primal force. The would-be killer was in the middle of making a second thrust when his body suddenly froze, shaking. As the knife fell from his grasp, he flew upward with bone-breaking force into the ceiling of the pod, only to be immediately released to fall limply on the floor.

Do you wish this one saved, as well? The great mind sent an image of Albert in similar trouble. Two professionals with knives were poised to open the young man's pod and make short work of him. Dante, panting, sent his frantic acknowledgement.

"Jack! Albert!" Dante said verbally as he spoke mentally to the Great Mind, urging the ship to be discreet. Jack understood immediately and left him to untangle himself from cables and crown, not caring if the equipment was damaged in his haste. He rushed to the platform and then to the adjoining pod in time to see Jack dealing with the last of the hitmen. A woman embraced Albert, her back to Dante.

"Albert!" he called. He nearly lost what little composure he had left when the two broke their embrace and turned to him.

"Thank you," Mercedes said. "Thank you for saving my son!"

CHAPTER : 20

The skimmer slid into line behind the others like a chain of fireflies floating toward the same destination. Everyone of importance had been invited to tonight's party and by the look of the conveyances, not a single person had declined the offer.

Albert was boyish in his admiration for the Captain of the *Monte Cristo,* and Mercedes watched affectionately as he tried to hold his father's attention as they skimmed toward the ship.

"You'll be as amazed as I am. I've really never met anyone like him!" The glow of yellow lights from the skimmer made him look younger than he was, and his enthusiastic smile only added to it.

"Not anyone?" Fernand asked drily. His fingers flicked through a hologram only he could see as he checked the latest Bacrarrae results. Mercedes clenched her jaw and turned away from the tableau. He couldn't even bother to get excited about his son's savior. "It's his own fault getting into that situation," was all he'd said when he'd arrived on station the next day. Likely, he was even jealous of the Davrini Hacken—it didn't take much to pique Fernand's jealousy. Wasn't that why she'd had to give up most of her career, slicing it down to the

119

barest of hours? He couldn't bear to play second fiddle to anyone.

"His benefactor has invited us to a party on his ship," Mercedes had told him with indifference the night he'd returned, although she felt anything but.

"What does that matter to me?" Fernand had asked.

"I thought you came here to win better trade agreements for Mondego Industries. I would have thought an ally from Davrini Hacken would be too much to pass up."

"Davrini Hacken. Hmmm. Good thinking, my dear. You were always good for that, at least. You don't think he's trying to steal Mondego Industries out from under me, do you?"

Mercedes had been cowed into silence. The "at least" still stung as she looked out over the panorama of the strange ship *Monte Cristo*. Her lines glowed with lights and holographic dancing art, and within... who knew? A mystery, for certain.

Mysteries and novelty were hard to come by these days. The surgical world was really just a human assembly line of repairs—her husband knew that well enough to have lost all respect for her position, despite the wealth it had given them, and her son was following directly in the path Fernand had set.

It was as if she could see the course of her days laid out before her as surely as that string of

120

skimmers in line toward the *Monte Cristo*. They were beads on a string that ended in her eventual death, each the exact same as the last. What wouldn't she give for just one more taste of the excitement that used to fill her days? She swallowed, clearing any sign of her thoughts from her face, and turned to smile lightly at her son.

"I'm sure he's wonderful," Mercedes agreed. They were all dressed in the latest fashion, which was a throwback to a style from ancient Earth. Women wore romantic, silk dresses with artful draping and a cut that suggested heaving bosoms from some anachronistic romantic period. The men wore tailored, dark clothing that looked military in cut.

"The *Monte Cristo* is said to be unlike any ship ever made. A ship of wonders," Albert said, his eyes glowing. "I can't wait to see inside. The Captain promised me a personal tour. No one else has been promised anything like that. No one else knows anything about him, except for me."
Mercedes smiled indulgently. They were almost at the head of the line.

When their turn to board came, the skimmer edged up to the ship's hatch. Both the hatch and the skimmer were within the artificial atmosphere of the space station, and it was almost enchanting to step from the open deck of the skimmer to the open door of the ship.

O   n either side of the door, men stood at attention, their clothing perfect demonstrations of Davrini Hacken attire and their pock-marked, scarred faces the only thing marring the vision it displayed. They must live very harsh lives in Davrini Hacken, not that anyone knew much about the place. It was said that they killed anyone who ventured into their space without a writ, and they granted no one writs beyond their border stations.

They stepped onto the hatch and one of the horrific visages looked directly in her eyes. "Fernand Mondego, Mercedes Mondego, and Albert Mondego?"

"Yes," she whispered, taken aback by his familiarity.

"Who else would we be?" Fernand asked drily.

"The Captain requested you be brought to him directly. He wishes to show you the ship himself."

One of the doormen peeled off, leading them into what must have been a cargo bay, although it was unlike any cargo bay Mercedes had ever seen. The holographics must have cost a fortune.

It appeared as though they walked on floating islands linked by chain-like bridges. The artificial gravity, however, must have been turned off and set for each island and stairway separately, because they wove in and out and up and down so those above them looked as if they were standing

122

upside down, while others looked as if they were standing at a complete right angle to Mercedes.. The sound of rushing water was everywhere, and tinkling waterfalls flowed in complicated arrays between the islands, weaving in and out of the dark like an Escher drawing. Colorful flowers floated on the flowing water and brightly-colored birds dove between the islands with water droplets shedding off their wings like falling stars.

Mercedes held her breath, her gaze tracing the chains and islands, until she thought she might grow dizzy. It was absolutely breathtaking and as novel as she could have hoped for.

"The holographics must have cost a fortune!" Albert said. "Look, there's the Captain!" He strode toward them with the confidence of a monarch and wore the exotic, flowing silk robe of the Davrini Hacken with tight black leather clothing underneath. An assortment of various-sized belts slung across his waist and low over his hips in a fashion that highlighted his anatomy just enough to make Mercedes' cheeks grow hot.

"A little flamboyant, don't you think?" Fernand always disguised his insecurity with criticism. Mercedes could sense him stiffen beside her, his pride already offended at the show the other man displayed.

"He's amazing." Albert's hero-worship reached a crescendo in the presence of its object, but

Mercedes couldn't object. Her thoughts echoed his almost exactly, if for different reasons.

She'd barely glimpsed him when he'd rescued Albert. He'd dashed in and out as if he were avoiding speaking to her. Now, here he was, the captain of a ship of wonders and absolutely exotic in appearance—especially with that patch over one eye.

"Like a modern-day pirate," Fernand said in an undertone.

"   Would you want him to hear you say that?" Mercedes asked. Really, Fernand's arrogance was going to sink him someday if he wasn't careful.

"What I want is everything he has," Fernand said, looking around at the wonders surrounding them. Mercedes could almost see the dollar signs tallying in his head as he took in waiters with drink trays, tables loaded with delicacies, and musicians scattered throughout the islands. One was lit with golden stars; dancing couples swooped across it in a manner that suggested the gravity was set to low on that particular island.

The Captain stepped onto their island with a welcoming smile on his roguish face. There was something so familiar about him, like a scent from childhood. Mercedes couldn't quite place it, yet it was there somehow. She fought with her memory, savoring the feel of it and trying to find it again. She was so caught up that she almost didn't notice

124

Villefort following in his wake. Fernand noticed, however, and nodded a greeting to the man.

"Talking about me?" the Captain asked with a grin. "Everyone is—but they are not my honored guests as you are.."

"Honored?" Fernand asked. His posture straightened, like his hackles were up. Fool man—as if he needed to feel threatened by a simple act of welcome.

"Of course," the Captain said. "There could be no party if I had not found success at Bacarrae, and there would have been no success without the genius of Albert Mondego. I'm honored to host his family tonight and honored to have been able to help you so much."

Fernand flushed and Mercedes tried to conceal her sinking heart. It wasn't like there had been much hope that her husband could tolerate competition, but now his pride would never allow him to truly ally with this man, no matter how much Mondego Industries could use the allegiance. That was the problem with pride: it closed far more doors than it ever opened.

Albert was flushed for a different reason, clearly pleased to receive praise from his idol. Just because Fernand was throwing away their chance to be close to the man didn't mean Mercedes needed to do the same.

125

She held out her hand with a smile. "Thank you so much for saving our son. We are in your debt."

The Captain took her hand in an outdated fashion and held it to his lips. The look in his eye pierced her, and for a moment, she wasn't sure if she should step closer or flee. Perhaps Fernand had been right to feel nervous. The fire in that single eye was enough to consume every dream she still had left.

"It was my pleasure," he said, and Mercedes' heartrate kicked into overdrive, beating twice as fast as usual. Her breath sped, her face heated, and she felt her tongue wetting her lips. Follow or to flee?

She took a step, involuntarily, toward him.

CHAPTER : 21

The Captain's smile turned almost intimate at her movement, but he released her hand and turned to Fernand and Albert.

"Count Mondego, Albert, I hope you will allow me to show you the *Monte Cristo*."

"She's fabulous, Captain." Albert tried to mask his enthusiasm, but Mercedes noted the tiny smile in the corner of the Captain's mouth. He knew he was adored by her son.

There was something about him that she couldn't put her finger on, like a name you've only temporarily forgotten. It was at the tip of her tongue, but every time she reached for it, it skittered back into the shadows. She frowned and noticed his dancing gaze was on her again.

"I dare say one ship is the same as another." Fernand made a show of looking around them, as if Escher mazes of waterfall and island were the norm in his day-to-day life. "I'll never say no to a new friend, though. Albert tells me you are a promising Bacarrae player."

"A talented amateur, more like," the Captain said, nodding to the other man with them. "Will you be joining us on the tour, Inspector Villefort, or have you represented the Company enough for one night?"

127

Villefort and Fernand locked gazes, and just as always, something passed between them that Mercedes wasn't able to determine.

"I'm afraid I'll have to decline, Captain. I'm sure my wife misses me—I don't like to leave her alone at a party," Villefort said. He coughed into his hand. "She wanders."

Mercedes watched her old shipmate carefully. He and Fernand seemed to exchange secret correspondence, but it was nothing her beloved husband bothered to inform her about. There was some puzzle there, if she could get to the bottom of it, but Fernand kept his affairs close to his breast and never thought it necessary to involve her. They must have been connected—they "bumped" into each other enough to make it hard to believe otherwise. She'd always thought it was just their shared secret, but was it more? Were they still silent allies?

Mercedes schooled her features to stillness, murdering the frown that threatened to emerge before it could appear on her face. Her husband's choice to exclude her in everything was not something she could do anything about. She had Albert and his future to worry about. He hadn't chosen her husband, after all, and shouldn't pay for her choices.

"Next time, then, Inspector." The Captain was all sophistication and grace—everything her husband was not. He smiled at his remaining guests. "This way, if you please."

Mercedes followed him across the island and to a regular-looking ship hatch. As they left the party and entered the ship, her son's smile grew. He followed close on the Captain's heels, and where Fernand's eyes weighed and measured everything he saw, Albert's open delight saw nothing but his new friend.

"Our banquet hall," the Captain said with a smile, opening a door and offering Mercedes a hand. Fernand swooped between them. "Don't trouble yourself, Captain. I'm sure I can attend to my wife." When he took her hand in the Captain's place, Mercedes blinked back her surprise. When had he last touched her, even casually? Had it been this year? She didn't think so. Yet, here he was, swooping in possessively. If someone had hinted yesterday that this might happen, she would never have believed them. She raised her eyebrows in question, but he ignored her, dropping her hand to follow the Captain. What had caused his sudden burst of territorial instinct?

"Will we see the bridge, Captain? I'd love to compare it to the ships I've served on," Fernand said.

"I'm afraid not, Mr. Mondego—the bridge is not a part of the tour—but here is our propulsion system."

Before they could go in, Fernand's eyes widened as he received a message. He flicked his

129

hand in the holographic display, pursing his lips in displeasure. He turned to Albert, all business.

"Your next game has been called, and so has mine."

"Excellent! I can't wait," Albert said. "Are you ready for more action, Captain?"

The Captain opened his mouth to answer, but he was cut off by Fernand addressing his son."We need to talk seriously about what moves you are authorized to make on behalf of Mondego Industries," he said sharply.

"You're among friends here," the Captain said with a smile. "Speak your piece."

Fernand started, as if he had forgotten the Captain was leading them on a tour. He shook his head, his expression wary.

"I thank you, Captain, but our business is private. In the coming games, we won't need your assistance. The great games are serious business. Come on, Albert—we must leave immediately. Thank you for your hospitality, Captain. I'm sure we'd be pleased to entertain you in turn… another time."

"We'll miss the tour," Albert protested.

"I'll take you on a tour whenever you like," the Captain said with a smooth smile.

"Tours be damned. This is Bacarrae." Fernand's eye had more focus than Mercedes had seen in years. Were this year's games of particular significance? It wasn't like he'd ever tell her.

130

"I'll have one of my men show you to the skimmers." The Captain nodded to one of his men in the passage. He responded to the nod by stepping forward and standing to attention. "I'll take Dr. Mondego on the rest of the tour. There's no point in spoiling the evening."

Mercedes' heartbeat quickened. Maybe if she could get him alone, she could work out what made him so familiar. If she couldn't, well... she'd still have him alone, and there was plenty of appeal in that.

Fernand looked torn between the urgency of his business and his desire to keep claim on his territory. If he thought she would leave just to go home and sit on her own while they discussed business without her, he could think again. She crossed her arms and he sighed.

"Yes, fine," Fernand said, beckoning to Albert. "We'll meet again, Captain. I'm anxious to discuss with you the situation in Davrini Hacken."

The Captain nodded to him with a secretive look in his eye. His gaze followed them down the hall as they left. He had such a predatory look that Mercedes shivered. He started, as if he had forgotten she was there, but he smiled when he turned to her.

"Let me show you the propulsion systems. Even idling here in the station, they're a thing of beauty."

Mercedes allowed herself to smile as she took the arm he offered. As soon as her hand

131

touched him, she felt the hairs on her arms rise. Something about him and his glorious ship was like an echo in her mind. She couldn't shake the feeling that there was so much more beneath his surface.

Memories of a time before her marriage bubbled up. She'd been so independent. The idea of meeting a dashing captain and touring his ship would have seemed like nothing out of the ordinary. Was it only nostalgia that made her mind drift back longingly to those days? She'd tasted passion once, but that was before mercenary calculation had been forced to take her helm.

The Captain led her into another room, dark and warm. The light was so faint that she could barely see. She drew closer to his arm, afraid of stumbling in the dark.

"Are there no lights?" she asked, her voice barely above a whisper.

"There are lights, and they're worth seeing." He drew her in so close that she thought she could feel his heart pounding in his chest, but she must have been mistaken. Why would *his* heart be pounding wildly?

He placed her hand on a rail in front of her. Even then, she clung to him with the other.

"Stop," he whispered. "Just a moment and all will reveal itself."

"What do you think of when you wait in the dark?" she asked.

"I wonder what makes a person betray the one they love most in the world."

A stab of fear shot down her spine. Did he know her secret? But, no.No one from Davrini Hacken would have heard about her poor Edmond and his fate..

"Desperation," she breathed. The answer had flown out of her like a fly released from a bottle. She'd been waiting years to admit that to someone. Somehow, confessing it to him here in the dark made her feel close to him. She let herself lean against his support a little more.

Her eyes strained in the darkness, and then there was a blue pulse of light. It spread across the horizon like blue veins across a lung. The sensation of being within a living thing, open for surgery, swept over her. But that was ridiculous —they were within a man-made machine like any other. Yet, with each of the following pulses, blue rippling to aqua and then swirling greenish yellow, the feeling of being inside an organism increased. It was warm and humid, and as the light danced across the vast room, her eyes sought the Captain's single pupil, dilated in the darkness. She gasped as his lips parted and felt her own do the same.

"Mercedes," he whispered, his lips trembling. He looked like a ghost from her past. It was impossible, yet she felt an overwhelming urge to kiss him. This wasn't part of her pre-determined life—this was something she could reach out and take for her own.

She stood on her tip-toes, heart hammering every nerve in her body tingling with anticipation with risk. The man he reminded her of so strongly in the hazy dark was long dead—nothing but a dream that haunted her pillow. And yet,In this moment, it was almost as if she could kiss this living man and bring the specter back from the dead.

She reached her hands out, delicately, questioningly, and rested them on the breast of his belted leather shirt. His heart pounded beneath them. She licked her lips uncertainly, summoning the courage, and closed her eyes...

"Captain?" Light flooded the room as the door to the passage opened, banishing the flickering lights of the propulsion room and dispelling whatever madness had seized her.

CHAPTER : 22

"It's time for the display, Captain!" Jack said from the passage beyond.

Dante struggled to pull himself together. The feeling of her so near after all these years was almost enough to undo him. Hadn't he dreamed of her while he was in prison for all those years? Hadn't he seen her face again and again in his hopes for the future until the day he finally realized she must have been as much at the heart of his betrayal as his best friend, Fernand?

How long could she have waited before she married him? Not long—Albert had been born within a year of his incarceration. She'd leapt into another man's bed weeks, if not days, or hours, after he had lost everything. Dante gritted his teeth. He must not succumb to the feel of her hand against his hammering heart. He must not be melted by the look in her deep, dark eyes that were so like Albert's. They were the very same eyes that had seen him so many years ago—perhaps the only eyes that had seen him fully.

She'd said desperation would motivate betrayal. Had she been referring to him? What in the world could she have been desperate about?

He cleared his throat violently and stepped back. "Thank you, Jack. Would you care to accompany me to the entertainment, Ms. Mondego?"

Her eyes lingered over him, as if she longed to caress him in each place her gaze traveled. He had never expected that, after so long, she would still have such power over him. He could barely move under the promise of her gaze. It shot little tingles of anticipation through him, as if they had never been apart all these years.

"I must go," she said, her words coming too quickly, as if she felt it, too. "It's been a pleasure, Captain. I hope we will see you again. Perhaps tomorrow, at the tournament?"

"Perhaps tomorrow," he agreed, crooking a finger to Jack. "Would you show Ms. Mondego out?"

Jack nodded and took Mercedes' arm in his. She smiled and followed, leaving Dante in the hall clenching and unclenching his fists. He must not let her sway him.

Not if you want your revenge. The *Monte Cristo* understood this one human thing completely. *You should have it. Betrayal is worse than death. I'm fogging her more than the rest so she won't realize it's you. We can't afford to tip our hand.*

Dante frowned. *I didn't ask you to do that.*

Consider it a gift.

He clenched his jaw and strode back to the party, brushing off the attention of adoring admirers as easily as he shrugged off the constant probes by employees of the Company into the inner workings of the *Monte Cristo*. They could guess all they

136

wanted. When his revenge was complete, they
would have all the time they could want to speculate
while he was shaking stardust off his hull and
zipping off to the next quadrant. He knew the chinks
in their armor—they wouldn't ruin him like they'd
ruined others.

He felt a shiver of anticipation. Eighteen
years of planning, plotting, and daydreaming were
culminating in this final thrust. He'd studied
Fernand's eyes carefully when they'd met, but there
hadn't been even a glimmer of recognition. Even
Mercedes had no idea he was her former fiancé.
Perhaps the loss of his eye had been worth it, after
all.

I keep telling you it was good for you. A
worthy sacrifice.
His eye scanned the crowds edging to the sides of
the islands as they waited for the display the *Monte*
Cristo was about to launch. There! Villefort was not
far away. He squeezed through, letting his single-
eyed gaze clear a path for him as party-goers shrank
from the famed Davrini Hacken.

His only regret in this was Albert. The
young man didn't deserve the tragedy that was about
to descend. He was nothing like his father. But he
didn't really think that revenge could be cheap, did
he?

Worth the cost. What is one young man
compared to what they took from you?

137

The firefly lights faded and the islands descended into near darkness. The rush of the intake of breath from a thousand throats filled the room and silence descended immediately after.

Now? the ship asked.

Now, Dante agreed.

Around them, holo-works exploded like fireworks for the senses—not just bursting lights, but bursting with scents, music, and burst of colorful birds. The crowd gasped with delight as Dante positioned himself behind Villefort's right shoulder. He'd studied the man so carefully for so long, and here was his chance to finally plant the first seed.

"Don't turn around," he whispered in the dark. "Nod if you understand."

As the next burst lit the crowd, Villefort was still nodding.

"I know your secrets. I know every dark deal you've made to get where you are. I know who you betrayed—the betrayal that started all of your corruption. Edmond Dante," he whispered. When the islands went black again, he slipped away through the crowd before Villefort could turn around.
On the next burst, Dante glanced looked back over the heads of the audience to see Villefort scanning the crowd, his face as pale as a sheet.

CHAPTER : 23

"**A**nd we're back from that break brought to us by Mana Energy Bars. When you're feeling drained, recharge your batteries with Mana! Now, the interview that everyone's been waiting for—the interview we got first with the questions no one else has the grit to ask. You've seen him triumph again and again in the arena, the dark horse from Davrini Hacken known only as the Captain! Bring him on out!"
Applause.

"Hello and welcome to our show, Captain— or Mr. Captain. What do you prefer?"

"Captain is fine."

"I love you, Captain! I'll have your baby!"
Shouting from the crowd.

"It's not that kind of show, ladies!"
Laughter.

Dante remained silent.

"Hey, whatever gets the ratings up! Seriously, though, we have a long list of questions here—serious questions. The one that's at the front of everyone's mind, of course, is why the eye patch? Are you a pirate? Was there a terrible accident while you were making breakfast one morning? What's the deal? This is the answer everyone is dying to hear!"

"You have to give something of yourself, sometimes, to find something from your dreams."

139

"What an answer, hey ladies? That's some deep thought right there."

"It's the truth."

"Now, of course, we have to talk Bacarrae. New Rome is home to the Grand Tournament, and even though you were an unknown a few short weeks ago, you've already made your way from the preliminaries into the big leagues. We've got some footage here of you and your… partner—protégé?— Albert Mondego, toppling the powerful Red League for the entry spot. A huge upset! Was this your plan all along?"

"I came to win. I have a very specific prize in mind."

"Oh? Do tell!"

"That would ruin the surprise."

"More surprises from the Captain? No surprise there, hey folks?"

Laughter and agreement.

"Now, let's talk about Albert Mondego for a moment."

"If you must."

"Son of the industrialist Fernand Mondego and famed doctor Mercedes Mondego, you've really thrown a stone into that family's pool and caused some waves, so to speak."

"Meaning?"

"Of course, you know Albert will be playing for Mondego Industries during the Grand Tournament alongside his father, who received a bye

140

through the preliminaries. You've helped Mondego Industries along quite nicely. Has there been any offers from Mondego to play exclusively for their company, or are you planning and betting to take all that back?"

"I won't be aligning myself with any one company."

"Then you're prepared to meet Albert on the field of battle, perhaps against his father as, well, a Bacarrae champion?"

"If that's how the matches come out. Albert is a strong player, and I have no doubt his father is, as well. They will be interesting matches."

***

Fernand paused the news feed, the Captain's face intense alongside the gaudy talk show host. He was dressed in high Davrini Hacken fashion and cut quite the figure. Hair slick and an ornament eye patch with small jewels embedded along the strap, he was a dandy—or at least pretending to be. Fernand took a long drink from his glass. He went to take another, but found it empty. He held it out to be refilled by the automatic dispenser.

"What do you think of him?" Fernand asked the heavy-set man sitting across from him. "Is he a threat? Is he weaseling into my son's affection and pushing us into an alliance to force Mondego Industries into something?"

The man across the table drinking mineral water wore a pleasant, unconcerned expression, despite the sullen and steadily declining mood of Mr. Mondego. When he spoke, however, there was nothing pleasant about the rasp of his voice.

"Any man who can play like that is a threat. We play the game of games. Mondego Industries needs to secure the rights to the Eastward Lanes. Business has not been good, and despite everything our PR spins about your skill, Fernand, you've only won three of your last five. Your losses have not been insignificant."

Fernand nodded.

"There's also what happened to the Red League assassins," the big man said, his face keeping its pleasant, careful lines. "I didn't see the bodies, but I read a medical report. He and the men in his employ are no strangers to violence. One man may have been dispatched with an abnormally strong psychic attack."

"He'd have to be a strong psychic to play like he does," Fernand growled. "Few can manifest physically."

"Just so," the big man smiled, making his cup float gracefully for a moment before it came to rest again.

"I've arranged for you and him to be drawn on the first match," Fernand said slowly. "He's bloated with confidence now, crushing the Red League like he did. Finish him now, early, and we'll

142

be rid of him. I'd rather see Mondego Industries supported by people I know and can control than by some loose cannon. He could just as easily turn on us, no matter how much good he's done thus far."

"That must have been expensive—almost as expensive as my services."

Fernand eyed the big man, glowering over his drink. "Well worth the cost, I think, if I can remove him from the games. He is poison to Mondego Industries and to my son."

"I heard tell he has an interest in your wife, not that any man wouldn't. I also hear he might have her interest, as well. The Captain's party was very educational. This wouldn't have anything to do with that, would it?"

"The first match," Fernand growled. "Make sure he goes no further."

The other man didn't break his calm expression as he nodded. "So it shall be."

CHAPTER : 24

Dante's chest was warm with satisfaction. He watched through his remote viewer as Villefort opened the tiny golden box on his desk. The man's face paled as the holographic image expanded upward, mushrooming into a sphere of streaming data. It hadn't taken long, with the *Monte Cristo's* help, to find every illegal deal the corrupt clerk had made, every negotiation that went outside the rules, every bribe, and every lie that had sent an innocent to prison. It wasn't hard to find when you knew it would be there.

The data stream faded from view, leaving only a solitary sentence behind.

I know what you did.

Villefort shut the box with a snap, and Dante lowered the viewer, sinking down into his premier seat on D deck, where he watched from a recreational balcony. He let out a long, trembling breath. He did know what Villefort had done. He'd known and forced himself to remember every day he'd been locked in that tiny cell, all by himself, for year upon year upon year. He'd memorized the man's crimes, and slowly, like the movement of the stars above his asteroid prison, he had thought of what he would do if he ever saw Villefort again. After a while, it had changed to *when* he saw Villefort again. Revenge was one thing that would keep you alive when hope was long gone.

Now here he was, sitting on the floor of a private balcony in a pleasure park on the space station at New Rome, his revenge so close that its taste was on his lips. Everything in him longed to take a bite. Wait, Dante. Wait for the exact right time.

Why don't you think of yourself as Edmond? the ship asked. *Mercedes certainly does when she thinks back to the man you were.*

Edmond is dead.

Is he? I wonder...

Stop wondering and get back on task. We have a man to drive mad with his crimes.

That shouldn't be a problem. He was halfway there, already.

Dante stood, brushed himself off, and answered the *ping* of the door into this portion of the garden. Jack entered, followed by a droid carrying their drinks and lunch on a tray. They took the tray, sat at a floating table with an excellent view of the stream and palm trees, and dismissed the droid.

"It went well?" Jack asked.

"Exactly according to plan."

The young man nodded. "You've been called up for a match with seven others, including a member of Mondego Industries. It's not Albert—he's playing a different game during that time."

Dante nodded and looked off at the palm trees as if he were enjoying their waving fronds, but his mind was elsewhere. He was like a weaver, slowly winding the threads together and holding the tension just so until the very end. He just had to be careful not to pull any of the strings too tightly before the time was right.

"Are you sure you want this?" Jack asked gently. "I remember you from... before. You weren't the type to destroy another person."

Dante drummed his fingers on the table while picking at the fruit on his plate. What bent a man so far that he wanted to see his pain in the face of another? He knew, but could he explain that to someone who hadn't lived it, themselves?

"They think I'm dead. They think they killed me, and do they look sorry?"
Jack shrugged. "I don't know."

"They look fat and happy," Dante said, spitting the words in his bitterness. "They look prosperous and rich."

"What about Mercedes? You loved her once, and at the party..." Jack swallowed. "At the party, it looked like she didn't mind you all that much, either—and she didn't even know it was you."

"She's the mother of another man's son... and my betrayer. She makes me feel like a fool whenever I look at her. I never even suspected she meant to sell me to my tormentors."

146

"You could call it off, tell her who you are. She doesn't look happy with her husband. Perhaps…"

Dante leaned forward, catching the younger man's gaze. "You're the only friend I have in this world, Jack, but if you bring this up again, you're off my crew. I've been planning this for a long time and no one–not even you–is going to take this from me now."

"You know you won't really send me away, Captain," Jack said, but his eyes held concern. "Whatever your plans are, I'm your man."

"I'm glad you think so, because I have to bet rather heavily on this next round."

"How heavily, exactly?" He shifted in his seat, controlling his nervousness admirably.

"They required a bet of a lifetime of indentured servitude—a level-five bet specified by the Company. They've taken an interest in our success."

Jack wiped his hands on his shirt and looked around, even though there was no one there to watch him. "Remind me why we're doing this, again, Captain. Indentured servitude… it would be a kind of prison sentence."

Dante took a long drink and cleared his throat before counting on his fingers as he named them, "Villefort, Mercedes, Fernand. In this life or the next, I'll serve my revenge to them and make them eat it to the last morsel."

147

Jack swallowed, his fists tightening nervously.

"And don't worry—I didn't bet my lifetime," Dante said, taking a last swallow of his drink before standing and clapping Jack on the shoulder. "I bet yours. Enjoy the garden. It's booked for an hour. Put whatever you want on my tab."

CHAPTER : 25

Dante sank into the command chair and closed his eyes a moment. Lily, respectful of his small time alone before the match, stood silently at the door, crown at the ready.

This is the first game in which you face equals.

Equals? With you by my side, I doubt that.

You still have much to learn. The universe is wide; in it, you are nothing.

Even so, I will win and have my revenge.

Do not throw your care away. You are becoming strong, but I will not be a crutch.

"Your crown, sir," she said, "and might I add, even though I can't betbeing an employee, all my friends are betting on you to win—not just this match, but to win everything. We think you'll win everything."

She handed him the gold band, and he placed it carefully with a practiced movement.

He smiled at Lily as the connections came online. "That is a lovely necklace. It suits you."

Lily put a hand to her throat with a shy smile. "It came yesterday, delivered by a courier. There wasn't a name tag, but I can guess."

Dante only smiled. "Good deeds should be rewarded."

"The Red League are a pack of bullies, sir. Kick them where they won't forget!"

"I'll try not to disappoint," he told her as reality was substituted for the negotiation area of the arena.

Seven more players were present, along with the official. Dante had read everything there was to read about each of his opponents. All his plans hinged on his continued success in the games. At least he didn't have to face Albert, yet. He was starting to find it difficult to look the younger man in the eye, knowing he would betray him. How was it different from those who had betrayed him and sent him to prison? He suppressed the thought—this was no time for introspection.

Placed around the arena were a pirate, a merman, a dragon that looked almost feline, another elf lord with a laurel of greenery and wooden armor, what looked like an undead sorcerer, a crusader emblazoned with red crosses, and a human mage with a lightning storm caged on top of his staff. Dante knew the pirate would be set against the crusader and the dragon, their representative companies currently locked in a fierce take-over bid that would be determined by the results of this match. That left four to worry about, and of those, the undead sorcerer seemed the worthiest opponent.

"Gune is a long-time fixture in the arena," Jack had advised while reading from a dossier earlier that day. "He was a high-level executive who fell

150

from grace—a powerful psychic and former inquisitor. Now, he sells his services. He's a Mondego employee as of yesterday—an agent of Fernand's."

Dante had shrugged at the time, but now with the game moments from starting, he bent all his will toward the man. Who was this agent of Fernand's?

He was met with a sea of calm—no emotions and no thoughts, just tranquil waters. Dante frowned and tried a different approach, but there was nothing. The man was like a block of stone and no thought radiated from him.

The Captain, I presume? So good to finally meet you, the rasping voice grated into Dante's mind. *I knew you had talent, my boy, but I never dreamed it would be so potent.*

You seem different from the others I've faced.

I would hope so. This is the Grand Tournament, after all—the big leagues. Ah, what's this? Another mind close to yours? An aid, perhaps? That boy you keep as a lap dog? That won't do, not at all. This is a contest of wills between giants. Anything else would be cheating.

A wave of nausea passed over Dante and he physically lurched forward in his command chair from vertigo. For the first time since meeting with the Great Mind, Dante could not feel the *Monte Cristo's* presence.

151

*There we are, much better. A battle of…
well, I suppose it remains to be seen if we are
equals. May the dice land where they will, Captain.*

The other man was gone from Dante's mind,
then, and he was left alone while the official finished
the details of the agreement.

"The top two competitors from this match
will proceed and split the match winnings," the
knighted official droned on before raising his sword
in salute. "Luck to you all!"

Disoriented, Dante accepted the agreement
and retreated to his side of the field to prepare. What
kind of mind could remain so strong in the face of
his assaults? Since training with the Great Mind,
Dante had grown stronger and keener, but this other
man seemed by far his superior. He gritted his teeth
and focused his thoughts. Before, the Great Mind
had given him an extreme edge that few dreamed
possible, allowing him to counter every move before
it was made. Now he would need to rely almost
solely on his Bacarrae skills, along with keeping his
thoughts shielded from Gune.

I must win for my revenge to be perfect.
Dante focused his mind into a knife's edge, a
weapon. *I must win to make Fernand and Mercedes
pay. I survived years in prison without the mind of
minds—I will survive this.* With those thoughts
fueling his psychic reserves, he laid out his forces
and prepared for battle.

152

CHAPTER : 26

The arena was laid out as islands with deep water between them—a choice picked by the pirate player for its clear advantage. Dante entered his elf lord avatar quickly and activated his special ability almost instantly: summon mount. This time, he chose not to use the griffon his opponents were so used to seeing and instead selected a tall, armored elk with razor-sharp antlers. He chose against elven archers, as well, and drew up battle lines of fast scouts equipped with a hooded hawk and short bows, a few specialist magic users, and heavy, slow-moving living trees that would perform well in and out of water. These units would be a challenge for Gune's undead sorcery to corrupt.

Grim but satisfied, Dante carefully sent fast hawker units to scout. He kept most of his psychic energy for defense, lest Gune penetrate his thoughts and unravel his strategies. He kept in mind the six other high-level players he might encounter, each one possibly out for the glory of upsetting his winning streak.

Dante slowly moved his main forces up, walking his elk under the cover of the great, living trees while his scouts ranged wider. He came upon the pirate in a pitched battle with the dragon player and watched through the eyes of one of his scout's hawks.

Of course the pirate would have a ship, Dante thought as he watched the battle through the eyes of a scout. Two dragons hovered just out of range of canon fire as an elegant ship sailed between the islands. One of the dragons swept around behind the ship and dove down, away from the pirate's broadside.

He watched with a certain amount of fascination as the crew hauled on the sails and brought the big ship almost to a standstill, nearly capsizing her as she rolled in the turn, the bow pulling hard to the east and away from the diving dragon. The broadside guns came into play just as the dragon neared, and a full round of cannon fire was brought to bear with deafening efficiency. The dragon squawked, screamed, and then fell into the water, lifeless. Its companion stayed a moment longer before winging away from the battle. Dante brought his scout back; this wasn't his fight—at least, not yet.

Being brash and rushing into fights had suited him when he'd had every advantage, but now his greatest ally was gone. He reached out again for the *Monte Cristo*, but there was nothing. He forced himself to dwell neither on it, nor on Jack. He couldn't afford the distraction of worrying about the young man he had depended on for so much. He should have been more careful in his betting, but

154

then he wouldn't have had a seat in the game, at all. He couldn't have expected that he'd lose the help of the *Monte Cristo*, either. He'd just have to fight smarter.

He began crossing a narrow bridge, and a ripple in the water beside him was his only warning before the attack came.

Fish men surfaced in formed legions and threw tridents in a coordinated attack. Dante lost one of his trees in the first barrage and only managed a lack-luster response with one of the living trees scooping up a mermaid and ripping it in half before it could escape.

Not a good exchange, Dante thought, keeping an eye on the leaderboard and seeing himself fall nearer the bottom. He would have to do better than that to stay alive. The arena was against him, as many of his opponents were well-suited to fighting in or around the water. Except for his trees, the best that most of his units could do was hold their ground.

Words from a teacher filtered into his mind from so long ago that they seemed from a different life. "Every time you see weakness, turn it into strength." He couldn't defeat all the players in the arena and shouldn't even try, but maybe he didn't need to—maybe he didn't even need to fight them.

Quickly, he ordered his magic users to cast a speed spell on three of his scout units before taking direct control of the middle one. He left the rest of

155

his forces in a loose formation, slowly moving toward one of the larger islands after looting the tridents and equipping them awkwardly in branch-like limbs. They'd serve poorly as weapons, being more hindrance than help, but Dante had a plan. All the while, he kept a sharp eye out for any ripples and marked their location carefully when he saw them following behind, waiting to strike.

It didn't take him long to find what he was looking for: the storm wizard waged a bloody and very visual battle with the other elf lord. The wizard's units seemed to have electrical attacks and shot mass lightning at range while the elven units had a hard time weathering the brunt of the attack. Still fearful of Gune's mental prowess, Dante risked easing his defense for a moment to find the wizard's controller. Where Gune's mind had been a pool of placid water, this man was a raging hurricane of emotions and haphazard plans. The man might have been a great psychic, but the patterns of his mind spoke of madness. Dante carefully surveyed the twisting mass of thoughts from afar until he thought he'd gleaned what he needed. Pride was foremost in the man's mind—exactly what he needed.

Dante's kept his slower units moving warily toward the storm wizard, coming up from behind the other player. The ripples in the water appeared and kept pace with them; the merman commander knew he was safe from Dante in the water. This time, Dante didn't mind. Marching closer to the other

156

battle, he drew merman and storm mage closer together.

Still controlling the hawker unit, he held his breath and waited, carefully feeling out the thoughts of the other two players while trying to keep his own presence masked. He had yet to sense Gune, but that might not mean anything. If the other man was powerful enough to sever his connection with the *Monte Cristo*, then he might have been standing right beside Dante without him knowing. He had one of his trees pass a trident to the elf lord and readied his units for battle. The moment was almost here— he could feel it.

When it happened, everything occurred in a blink. The wood elf mustered his troops and, under cover from several expert archers, charged the storm troops. Dante used that distraction to charge his own elf lord up and over the small crest he'd been hiding behind toward the storm commander. It was a risky move, exposing his commander like that, but nothing else would do. The bait had to be valuable for his trap. He cleared the rise swiftly and threw the trident like a spear, just as the wood elves were beaten back into a ragged group.

The trident struck squarely in the back of a soldier guarding his commander, the tines digging deep into the unit's armor and felling it with one strike. Sensing an attack against his life, the storm wizard spun, furious, in time to see Dante's elf lord rear his battle elk and taunt him. He then ran back down the hill to relative safety.

"Insults!" the storm wizard screamed. "Insults will be answered in kind!" He enacted his special ability, a power called "storm call," and directed the massive thunderhead over the hill without aiming, trusting the storm to do its work.

Dante grinned and ran away atop his elk, hawkers following almost as swiftly keeping just ahead of the rolling wall of lightning. He commanded his trees to throw their tridents into the banks of the sea, like so lightning rods sticking up from the bank. The trees then fell to their sides. The mermen, sensing something coming, rose above the water long enough to see the massive storm wall and perish as great forks of lightning struck the long, metal shafts of the tridents. The merman army disappeared in the flashes and ear-popping crashes of thunder, their screams too faint to be heard.

Several of Dante's tree men had been struck and destroyed, as well, but the gamble had been worth it. The storm mage rose to the top of the leaderboard and two other sides all but disappeared; the wood elves were on the run and the mermen resigned from the battle, admitting defeat. The storm wall diminished and died, its power spent. As the remaining storm units crested the hill, they found a compliment of living trees in hiding, Dante's magic units casting protection spells on their already-hardy compositions, and as the trees waded forward all but

158

immune to the lightening attacks, there was one less opponent. His elf lord reversed his mad fleeing and charged back to the fray, the battle elk using antlers and hooves to thrash the enemy lines as his elven blade stuck out like a serpent.

When it was finished, Dante's avatar had supplanted the storm mage at the top. From the listings, the other half of the battle between pirates, crusader, and dragons had ended with a grisly loss of units; Gune's undead sorcerer had executed a coup de grace against the survivors.

There were only two players left. Dante set his mouth in a hard, thin line and prepared to meet Franklin Gune on the field of battle.

CHAPTER : 27

The battlefield was silent, save for the soft footfalls of Dante's war elk and the heavy *glup glop* of the tree units as they walked through the shallows and mud. He was no longer careful of the water, with the aquatic units all dead or sunk, there was no longer any reason to fear it. The battle to come would be one of force and determination—not subtle maneuvering. Gune's mind was a mystery. Yet, during the battle with the storm wizard, Dante had been spread out, engaged, and unable to thwart another attack. Perhaps Gune was in the same seat, grating his teeth for lack of information, but too professional to let his weakness show.

Dante's own latent talent had grown substantially since he'd discovered it, first under human tutelage during his time in prison and now with the teachings and power of the Great Mind. Just because he hadn't known Gune could cut his connection to the *Monte Cristo* didn't mean Dante couldn't defeat him.

I will not be a crutch. The statement had been the last thing the *Monte Cristo* had thought to him before Gune entered the picture.

"I am Captain of the *Monte Cristo*," Dante said to himself. "I do not need a crutch. I will have my revenge."

Revenge, hmm? Revenge puts a man in a dangerous state of mind. Some might say it's a defenseless state. Very dangerous.

Gune's voice continued to grate inside Dante's head. He felt the calm pool of the other man's thoughts and knew he was close. His own units were masked, as were his opponent's, but there was little left to do than test each other's mettle. Their psychic powers stood at a stalemate.

The center island looks a good place to settle this.

Only a fool would let his opponent choose the field of battle.

Dante sent the feeling of a shrug. *Suit yourself. I'll be waiting.*

He set his units in motion, a slow and alert group ready to engage and guarding against surprises. All the bridges and fringe islands somehow led to the center of the arena and Dante let the natural layout of the arena guide him. He passed the other battle site, with bodies strewn here and there, their broken forms the refuse of war.

As real as the visuals looked projected into his mind from the crown, he knew them to be false and could clearly see the tell-tale signs of artificial construction. He pitied what they represented, in a detached way: lost fortunes and squandered life. Fernand was at the forefront of his mind. He kept him there like a beacon, angry, red, and leading him forward. The years in prison had done nothing to

161

dull the sting. He used his revenge as a mask; all Gune would be able to see was his hatred.

Fernand Mondego? He's wronged many, to be sure, and you're among good company with your hatred of him, but why?

Dante stayed quiet. He assembled his forces and waited. Gune crested the hill moments later with skeleton knights on zombie horses and other undead monstrosities. The sorcerer leader rode a skeleton dragon; its bony wings were not able to fly, but the creature was no less dangerous. Dante realized Gune had gained his dragon mount by using his special ability, "raise undead," on one of his opponent's dragons. At least he couldn't use it again, Dante thought, although it was small comfort.

Your skill at the game is obvious, as we're the only two left, Gune rasped. *Your intentions are obvious to me, as well. I'll detect your reasons soon enough. I was an inquisitor in my day, boy. What have you been?*

Dante pursed his lips. Gune's mind wasn't changing and was still an unreadable pool, but Dante started to see the edges of his influence. Gune was in his head, but when Dante sent his own thoughts ranging, the man couldn't be felt. *He's concentrating all his power in one place,* he realized. *He doesn't know how to split his focus.*

Memories of torture and hard lessons learned in Chateau D'If from the Abbe, his first real teacher, flooded back. The pain had been exquisite, but in time he'd learned to separate his mind—cordon it off—from the part being beaten and violated. The Abbe had helped and schooled him in the subtle arts, even as he'd filled his head with stories of the *Monte Cristo*. He would take those teachings and use them here, splitting his mind and hoping he was right that Gune couldn't focus on two different points at the same time. It was his only chance.

He split his mind in two and sent his second self with part of his units, breaking off to flank Gune's advancing forces under cover. There was something else, as well, that was happening outside the arena. He could feel millions of personae changing from entertained to collectively horrified. Gune noticed it, as well, and Dante felt the other man momentarily shift his focus away from his opponent to investigate.

In that moment, Dante struck. His flanking troops weren't yet in the best position, but he realized he wouldn't get another chance like this. He spent the rest of his spells on his tree units, increasing their speed and strength, and made them lumber forward. He kept pace with his elk, reining in so he didn't get ahead of his slower troops. His faster hawker scouts in the flanking force outpaced and came from the east, even as Dante realized what was happening outside: Villefort was climbing the maintenance scaffolds and catwalks of the arena. Dante reached out to his mind, feeling hints of guilt

163

dancing around the edges and despair washing through the man's entire psyche.

This was it: he'd pushed Villefort to the brink. What was wrong with that, though? Dante had never lifted a hand against him—never turned him over to the authorities to be sent to the hellhole he had finally escaped from. No, he'd only shown him a glance of himself in the mirror. Was there anything wrong with speaking the truth to a man?

Certainly not. It's only justice. The ship's mind was only connected to his for an instant to share his satisfaction, and then it was gone again. Gune must have been very powerful.

As his hidden self struck and his main force punched into the somewhat distracted forces of Gune's undead, Villefort reached the very top of the arena. He stood there for a moment on shaky legs, the battle raging below him. His face was ghostly pale, even from so far away, and he clung to the balcony with trembling hands.

Dante couldn't tear his eyes away from the specter.

Villefort threw his head back, like he was pulling together courage, and then let out a wild cry accompanied by a psychic wave that echoed and punched through the minds of anyone nearby. It reverberated through the Bacarrae tank, wave upon wave of pain and despair echoing through the game field. Gune faltered, shutting his mind off from the wave, along with his connection with his troops.

Dante felt the effects, as well, but the part of himself he'd fractured away was safe, protected, and secure, and its troops continued their onslaught.

He sucked in a breath as he felt a shift in Villefort's mental vibration. It hardened in resolve, and then he jumped from the highest point of the arena. His body star-fished out, like he thought he could grab the air with his stiff limbs, and then corkscrewed as he fell to the arena below. He hung in the air for long seconds, each stretching to infinity as the inevitable grew closer. The fall took long seconds, but so short compared to the years of desiccation Dante had suffered at his hands.

He let the man's final psychic cry wash over him. This was his revenge, and it was glorious and horrible and wonderful. He flinched from the guilt of it, even while feeling a grim satisfaction that it was done. He'd uncovered every sordid deed Villefort had ever committed—every back room deal and betrayal starting, of course, with his own. There was no need to shy away from the truth. For nearly two decades, he'd suffered from Villefort's choice. The man had done this.

As Gune recoiled from the psychic blast, Dante struck. Gune's units came forward, leaderless and listless, and fell effortlessly as his own troops marched forward. The flanking maneuver he'd prepared to even the odds was now overkill; the other man's vanguard was crushed and the skeleton dragon that had seemed so powerful before could not stand against the forces he brought to bear. As Gune came back to his senses, his commander began to flee, boosted by the haste spell "ghost." Dante sent his avatar in pursuit, the only unit fast enough to catch him. The battle was all but finished.

You need no crutch. Monte Cristo's mind was suddenly back in Dante's head, the alien a reassuring presence.

Gune lost his control?

That human? No human could shut me out! I left to test you. You are becoming yourself, slowly. I shall reveal all of you to yourself, yet.

A test?

You learned much.

The ship's voice, however, was interrupted by a desperate cry. *Help! Dante, can you hear me? Please, someone! Please!*

The mental voice of the cry stabbed through him. Albert was in trouble! That would have been enough to worry him, but the cry resonated with him. It vibrated in his mind so his thoughts buzzed with it like a string beside a tuning fork. Albert's mind, which had opened completely in this vulnerable moment, matched his in impossible ways. It was like a thinner version of his own, void of the scar tissue of years in prison. He felt an immediate and overwhelming need to protect him like nothing he'd felt before.

Dante's head whipped around. He needed out of the simulation. He needed to get to Albert.

166

I'm coming! He shouted back with his psyche, hoping the answer would reach the boy and give him some sort of hope as he ran to save him.

Not now! the *Monte Cristo* insisted. *Now, we win!*

He needs me. I cannot refuse him.

What about Jack? You play for his indenture. Albert is the son of the enemy!

Dante's head spun. Gune and victory was just ahead, but Albert's life hung in the balance. If he left now, he would forfeit and lose Jack's freedom. If he didn't, Albert would lose his.

He'd just have to risk it. If he lost Jack's freedom, he could win it back. If he failed, he, his crew, and the *Monte Cristo* could strike at whoever took Jack and steal him back, blast out of the system, and hide in a backwater somewhere. He didn't need to worry about that now. No, right now, he was powerless to do anything but run to the Albert's aid.

You realize what this means, don't you—this resonance?

Yes, he answered the ship.

CHAPTER : 28

Dante snatched the halo off his head, leaping from the chair.

Forfeit, said the writing on the wall in bright, blinking letters. Lily stood beside it with a hand over her mouth. She'd bet on him to win, Dante remembered—another person he was disappointing—but he couldn't think of that now. He let the halo fall to the floor and dove for the door. Skidding through the halls, he sped to find the other arena in the low lighting and coolness of the players' level.

There it was! He scanned the leaderboard noting the game was almost complete. The game bet was a level six: the loss of your life, or the life of someone you cared about. Knowing Albert, he had bet his own.

Why had he bet such risky stakes? Was Mondego Industries so callous that they would risk the life of the heir? Fernand was a cruel master and a crueler father, but this...

Dante smacked his hand hard against the holo, skipping past the formalities and registering his own late bet. He'd start with a penalty and have only a quarter of the resources of the current game leader, but it was his only chance. With shaking hands, he selected the option to let him play on

Albert's team, their victory shared if they achieved it.

Once everything was confirmed, he leaped through the door as soon as it opened, jumping past the holographic greeter who sought to confirm his entry and into the only player room with an open door. An attendant was cleaning the halo.

"I'll take that." He snatched it from her hand, ignoring her startled cry, and jammed it on his head, wincing as it made the rough connection. His thoughts raced as the program connected. He had a son. Family. Blood of his blood. Mind of his mind. They'd hidden that, too. Somehow, his pain of betrayal stung a thousand times worse at the understanding that he'd been robbed of a treasure he'd never even known he had. They'd taken everything from him: his future, his freedom, his friends, his lover… his son.

He bit hard on the inside of his cheek to force his thoughts to focus. This was no time for pain or grief—he was about to lose the boy before he even knew him for who he was and nothing could make him allow that.

If you do this, you'll have no help from me. We're here for one reason only, and it's not to rescue bastards.

He's my son!

Dante leaped into the game, his mind searching the landscape in great sweeps. He couldn't afford to take the best strategy; he could only afford to find his son. There!

He drove his full force at top speed toward the hill where Albert's single remaining unit stood and fought. The young man was surrounded by enemies, and their forces far outnumbered Dante's. Even from here, he could see Albert's unit was flagging. He had only moments.

How could he save him? There was no way he could come up with a strategy that drew the battle away from Albert in time. He watched an enemy unit strike Albert's with a critical hit.

"Dante!" he cried as his unit flashed a warning. One more strike was all it would take.

Dante swallowed, feeling fear pulse through him. He couldn't allow his son to die before his eyes, pleading with him for salvation. He'd rather go back to prison—he'd rather let them betray him all over again.

He screamed mentally at his enemies, throwing all his psychic weight behind it. They must be stopped. They. Must. Be. Stopped.

The enemy units froze mid-stride. All three of the opposing players' units were stuck in place, unmoving. Dante gasped—his head screamed in pain. What had he done? How had he frozen them? It didn't matter; his units crashed into the enemies until there was nothing left but Albert looking shocked.

I did say you had the potential to do more.

171

The game announced them winners, but it wasn't enough. He had to be sure Albert was alright and that there wasn't a misunderstanding or hidden penalty. He mentally threw himself back into his body, snatched the halo from his head, and dashed past the horrified attendant.

There! One of the rooms had Albert's name on it. Dante flung open the door as the boy's eyes opened. He was alive. Alive! His brown eyes—so like his mother's—looked back at him and Dante fought to control his own expression. How could he have missed it? He must have been blinded by his desire for revenge, because now he couldn't stop seeing himself in the boy. AThe look in his eye—relieved, but confused—told Dante his son could sense something, too.

"Albert!" Mercedes flew into the room, anxiety flooding her expression. "I was watching the game. I thought all was lost."

"Mother," he allowed her embrace.

That moment between mother and son was too much, and Dante spun and fled the room, returning to his own, with his breath heaving in his chest. He needed to slow down and pull himself together.

The attendant, stunned, still stood where he'd left her.

"They all froze," he said, glaring at her as if she could explain it.

She shook, but tapped her implanted communications system and said, "The other competitors were found unconscious in their chairs. Whatever you did—"

"A moment of privacy, please." His tone was sharp; he didn't need to hear either applause or scolding from her. She left, taking the halo with her.

He clutched the head of the chair, trying to suck in a breath, the sight of mother and son still etched across his retinas. That should have been his. His betrayers had taken that from him, too.

CHAPTER : 29

Dante flexed his hands, trying to keep his brain from spinning. It all added up. Albert was eighteen years old and Dante had been imprisoned nineteen years ago. Psychic ability was hereditary—even before he had been imprisoned, Napoleon had claimed he was a strong psychic.
He ran a hand through his hair and sucked in a deep breath. He'd bent almost double to lean on the wall with one hand. Now that he had a moment to think, it was all crashing in on him.

He's your son. The *Monte Cristo* was as sure as he was.

He'd liked the boy from the moment he'd met him, but now something protective and fierce had blossomed in his heart. There must have been a way to keep him out of the events Dante had set in motion—to keep him safe. He just needed time to think.

It's too late. Now that you've begun, you can't stop.
The ship cared nothing for mercy, but there was always a way if you took the time to think it through.

He'd escaped from prison, hadn't he? He'd assembled a crew of men who had been intent on killing him. He'd found the *Monte Cristo* and

174

watched Villefort fall to his death—the perfect revenge. There had to be a way to get this, too.

He felt a touch on his shoulder and shied away from it like an injured beast. Looking up, his head still whirling, he saw her: Mercedes. Her hand rested on his shoulder, her eyes concerned and deep with emotion.

"Are you injured?" she asked.

He shook himself, fury filling him at what she'd stolen. What had she been thinking when she purposely betrayed the father of her son? Suddenly, it was as if a missing piece had clicked into place. She'd been pregnant when she'd betrayed him. She'd been carrying—protecting—his son. She'd done it for Albert, too.

Her smile was tentative. "I came to thank you for saving my son… again. What would we do without you? I will cover the cost of what you lost and gladly give you whatever is in my power to give."

He swallowed, because now when he looked at her, he saw the woman he once loved. The protective stone of his heart cracked a little. Desire tore through him, laced with the hurt of betrayal. She was still his Mercedes and the mother not of Fernand's child, but of his. Somehow, that made her more precious and the horrible pain of loss more powerful.

He reached for her, roughly pulling her to his chest. His breath was ragged, and her eyes grew large and dark in response. She didn't stop him when he kissed her long and hard, like he was taking what was his. Wasn't she his? Shouldn't she still be his?

Her arms wrapped around him and she pressed her soft body against his. The memory of what used to be filled him, and he closed his eyes, letting himself sink into her kisses and caress, just as he had in the past. Was she was kissing him in her relief at her son's salvation or because she could somehow sense it was him, her Edmond, after all these years?

His hands dipped under her shirt, exploring her skin and feeling the silky smoothness that hadn't changed over the years. He was losing conscious thought in the feel and smell and taste of her, his desperate need for her mixing with the agony of what he had lost.

What he wanted was his nineteen years back. He wanted them to have been with her and their son. He wanted this moment to bring them all back and finally give him what was his by right.

She moaned in his arms and his fingers dug deeper, holding her tightly against him. He slipped his hands under her bottom and hitched her up from the ground, sucking in a breath and desperately keeping back a cry of pain. Her presence hurt him— her closeness reminding him with every touch of what could have been—but at the same time, he wanted all of her. He turned her so her back was to the wall and deepened his kiss, leaning into the hurt. She gasped, breaking the kiss for a moment.

"Anything you want is yours," she whispered.

"This?" he asked.

"Yes. Please, yes."

He couldn't let this happen, though, could he? Not again. Hadn't she seduced him the night before she betrayed him? He should tell her who he was and let her feel the anger and bitterness that still wrapped around his heart and mixed with the powerful longing.. He should tell her exactly what he thought of how she had treated him and let her feel a fraction of the pain he'd borne. He couldn't yet expose himself, but he needed to say something to make her feel the way he did.

"He's betting with his life, you know—your son's life," he said softly. "Your husband cares so little for you that he bets the life of your son in these games, all for positioning."

She bit her lip. "I know."

"Is that why you're here? Is this nothing but revenge for you?" He spat the words, confused about whether he was angry at her, at himself, or at both of them, or if he just wanted to take them back and let this intimacy last a moment longer..

The ship dropped the mask so suddenly that Dante gasped, dropping his hold on Mercedes. She stumbled backward against the wall, her eyes wide

177

as she clapped her hands over her mouth and her eyes filled with tears.

"Edmond?" she whispered.

His lips parted, but there was a lump in his throat and he couldn't respond in time.

"Mercedes?" The warning tone in Fernand's voice as he entered the room made his wife stand straighter, her hands dropping to her sides. She was mussed, her hair out of place and her neckline tugged to the side.

Fernand couldn't have heard her words, but her demeanor gave her away. Her gaze darted from Dante to her husband and back.

His mouth formed a tight line as he took her arm in one hand.

"I think it's time for my wife to go. Her son needs her," Fernand Mondego said calmly, steering her toward the door. He paused just before they went through. "But don't think I didn't catch a glimpse of the two of you. Mondego honor has been challenged and that challenge cannot be ignored."

"No, Fernand, he saved our son!" Mercedes protested.

Fernand's voice was almost a growl. "I challenge you to Bacarrae of the highest stakes!" Dante frowned, drawing a breath. It was one thing to plan to bait a man, but another thing entirely when he bit. Now, to tighten the line.

"What bet?" he asked.

Fernand laughed harshly. "Everything."

"What?" Dante asked quietly. He must not look too eager.

"Everything I have against everything you have, Davrini Hacken. All worldly possessions and all family, employees, and crew, including that man of yours Mondego Industries just won as a slave. If it's not for everything, then it's just a game. I will see you ruined!"

"I'm lucky when it comes to games," Dante said.

"Don't count on it. Your luck left on the last transport. It's just you, me, and Bacarrae now, Captain. "

CHAPTER : 30

The official was finishing up the final tally at Company Headquarters. Personal bets were handled on terraces beside a massive water display. Between intricate mermaids spewing water into the air was a small holographic display and a smug-looking official in Company uniform. All of Dante's other matches had Company-mandated bets; this was his first time at the headquarters, and his skin crawled from being so close to the governing arm of the Company. Someday, someone would have to do something about them. Perhaps that might be his goal, when all this was over.

The Company shared his aversion as officials watched them carefully, hostility in their expressions. So much for their desire to see the Davrini Hacken pleased. They looked like they would tear him apart right now if they could, and every so often, one of them would nod to Fernand as if he were doing them a favor. Was he?

Not to my knowledge. This is personal for him, just like it is for you. His company is in peril, his son worships you, and you would have destroyed his top enforcer if you hadn't forfeited. His wife was the last straw.

"Mr. Mondego has bet against everything you have, Captain Monte Cristo. Our tallies of your worth, based on the value of your ship, your crew, your credit account, and your life, are very close to the estimated worth of Mr. Mondego when you include Mondego Industries, his employees, and his family. His own life is deemed a tiny fraction more than what you bring to the table, so it is not included in the bet. The game is set to be Bacarrae Mortalis, full immersion and pain simulation. This has been agreed to by both parties."

Fernand's eyes went wide, his face paling as the blood rushed from it. Dante clamped down on a grin. So, Fernand had not realized how valuable his holdings were. He'd bet blindly, thinking Dante's all-in could not possibly be worth enough to worry about. The tables had turned, it seemed.

All those years ago, he had taken everything from Dante, except his life. Now, if Dante won the match, the stakes were the same and he would take everything from Fernand, except his life.

"You have agreed to the terms by your thumbprints before the tally," the official said. "Good luck in your game."

He left before Fernand was able to pull himself together enough to reply.

**

Dante stalked through the holds of the *Monte Cristo*. A moment earlier, he'd sent out the all hands call; now his crew was assembling in the holds. They knew what had happened—they knew of Jack's fate. Dante had only had a moment to talk with Jack before the agents of Mondego Industries had taken him away.

"I plan to get you back," he'd said. "I just need to win this battle with Fernand. Your freedom is part of the bet." Dante had grasped Jack by the arm. The young man was a turmoil of emotions, but he'd returned his Captain's grip.

"You're betting with my life again." He'd showed no emotion on his face, but his dead tone had said it all. Loyal or not, he felt betrayed by Dante's actions.

The older man had swallowed. "I owe you an apology. In the middle of the game, I found out Albert is my son. I couldn't watch him die when I could do something about it. I just had to try..." Jack had nodded, comprehension dawning on his face. "So, this time it wasn't about revenge."

"And it isn't this time, either. I'm going to win your freedom back."

Jack had shaken off his grip. "Don't say it isn't about revenge. I'm a side bonus—the main meal is revenge on Fernand. Don't pretend it's not something more."

Dante looked away. "What do you want me to say? This is all I've had for twenty years."

"I want you to say it isn't all you have now. You have a friend who needs you, a crew, and now a son. Maybe that could be enough."

Dante had run a hand through his hair. Could it be enough? He'd shaken his head. "Even if saving you didn't mean fighting him…"

"You'd still need the revenge." Jack frowned. "Just remember: when your hunger is insatiable, you end up eating yourself, too.

"Meaning?"

"If you're not careful you'll lose what little humanity you still have. Stop this madness before it's too late. You can come out of this without regrets, Captain. There's still time."

"I'll think about it."

His loyalty is beyond anything you deserve. Although his concern for your humanity is misplaced. What makes humanity a trait worth embracing over revenge?

He's proven himself beyond a doubt, whether I deserve it or not.

Dante brought his mind back to the present, to the door in front of him that led to the hold where his men were gathering. He took a steadying breath and pushed it open.

"Captain present!" Sleeveless Bill called, and the crew came to attention. A stab of pain flashed through him as he realized that job had been Jack's.

Dante surveyed them. He'd worked beside them under the command of Captain Roberts, commanded them when he'd taken over *Schrodinger's Feline,* and he'd led them here, to

183

discover something wondrous and powerful. He'd promised them riches, but that's not why they followed him. These were the men who had seen him walk into the eye of the Great Mind and emerge as something more—something powerful.

"Friends, the journey I started so long ago is nearly at an end," Dante started, looking at each of them. "I haven't always asked, but I've always known you would all follow me wherever I went."

"Of course, Cap'n," Bill said. "None of us could have seen what we saw and not followed you. You challenged the dragon, so to speak, and found the treasure."

"I did," Dante agreed with a sad smile, "but my reasons were mine alone, just as this revenge is mine alone. Now I've been challenged in the final fight to take everything from my enemy and utterly destroy him, but it could cost me everything. He's wagering everything in his influence against my fortune, the *Monte Cristo,* and all of you. If I lose, I will lose everything."

The crew grew silent for a moment.

"You'd get Jack back, then, when you win?"

"Yes."

"Would you get that boy you keep saving, too?"

"If I win, yes."

Bill nodded. "Seems to me you're the best Bacarrae player the galaxy has seen in a long time—maybe even since Napoleon. Hell, if you and

184

Napoleon were to square off, take off the gloves so to speak, I don't know where my money would land. What's at stake is powerful motivation."

Dante nodded. "That it is."

"Seems to me you can't lose, Captain, with only that Fernand Mondego against you. He can't be as good as all that,"

"He's become a master at the game," Dante said, "although most of his plays happen off the field. He's underhanded, ruthless, and never plays fair. He's been run up against the Bacarrae board a number of times, but he's always managed to counter the charges brought against him. His mercenary, Gune, was a master psychic, but Fernand will be my most powerful adversary."

Bill surveyed the crew while scratching the stubble on his jaw. "Well, we'd better all get box seats for the show, then, hadn't we, Cap'n? You'll be paying for them, of course."

It is a great man who can foster such loyalty. I chose you correctly.

"Does Bill speak for all of you?" Dante called out to the room.

There was resounding agreement—a chorus in the affirmative. Dante felt his heart move, a dangerous feeling when he'd been so often consumed the by rage and bitterness that fueled his revenge. This was more, though—this was the dedication of a family to a father who may have made some wrong decisions in the past, but who

185

nevertheless still inspired his children. In their eyes, he could do no wrong.

"I'll make the preparations," Dante said, "and one way or another, we will finish this."

CHAPTER : 31

A hawk screamed overhead, so life-like that Dante could have sworn it was real. When they'd said this would be a more immersive experience, they hadn't been joking.

"This is common?" he'd asked Lily as she hooked him into the full bio-response rig, attaching patches to various points across his body. "Can't the room read my biometrics?"

"Yes, it can," she'd said. "These are to simulate pain."

"Only simulated?"

Her eyes had been sad when she'd replied. "It makes no difference. Enough of it and you'll overload and die of a heart attack or fall into a catatonic state. I've seen both."

"Ah."

"They're not common, but they do happen. If the participants request it, they can go full-immersion. Usually, it's a grudge match. Full immersion matches are always a crowd pleaser, and with your bet today, there won't be a place to stand on the observation deck. Trust me when I say if you survive this, you'll be all anyone can talk about. Are you really betting everything on this match? Everything?"

"It says it on the board, doesn't it?"

Now here he was, standing in the game, leading his units in the last great Bacarrae battle he ever expected to fight. The game would start in two minutes, and they were frozen until it began. After that, it was only his skill and passion against Fernand's. Either he'd walk away with everything he still wanted in the universe, or he'd be dead.

He could almost taste his victory, but the echo of Jack's words was still in his mind. Was he eating himself up in this insatiable drive for revenge? Was he losing his humanity?

Is someone thinking about losing? How fitting. Fernand's mental voice echoed in his mind. He was surprised by how recognizable his old friend's voice was. It was like a mental echo of who he was. Dante felt his thoughts focus at the feel of it.

You're always losing, Fernand Mondego, because you don't know what you have. Friends, family—they're nothing but pawns to you, aren't they?

What do you know about my friends?

I know you don't seem too shaken up about your old crony, Villefort, taking his own life.

I hardly knew the man.

That's not what the evidence I have of cheating the Company shows. The two of you were so deep in your embezzlement that it would take a full division of forensic accountants to find all the little leaks going from the Company and into your pockets.

188

Ah. So, it was you who drove Villefort to jump. Interesting. If you expect me to make your job here easier by offing myself, think again. If you had real evidence, you'd have gone to the Company and dealt with me through official channels. I'm calling your bluff.

Oh, I don't work for the Company. Their punishments are too good for you.

Ten more seconds and the game would start.

Who do you work for, then?

Five more seconds. Dante took a deep breath. It was time for the fight of his life.

When we meet face to face, I'll tell you.

His thoughts focused and he was in the game like he'd never been before. There wasn't a choice, this time, and he was the elf lord, cemented to the unit's health and actions. His beloved avatar was him, for this battle, and their fates were firmly entwined. Fernand, he knew, would be playing as his iconic night guild assassin—ironic that their two sides so closely mirrored their respective personalities. Dante chose a complement of archers, woodland knights, and two elven wizards with flaming staffs. Fernand loved shadows, sneak attacks, and deflection; Dante would burn through the shadows, reveal himself, and destroy his foe.

The arena was woodland grown up through old ruins, a landscape that benefitted them both in equal measure. Dante's woodland elves could easily hide and move through the trees while Fernand's

189

assassins had bonuses in the city. For once, at least, the tables weren't slanted to begin with.

He moved forward, the bio-sensors causing him to feel the wind on his face, and he shivered, feeling cold. If he'd woken with no memories in this place, he might have believed himself to be King of the Woodland People. His units surrounded him, although they moved silently. There was only the sound of the wind and the trees.

Out there, somewhere close at hand, Fernand was hiding and waiting for him. He couldn't have known Dante would be his undoing. He close his eyes while walking and stretched his mind out like a net. He'd repelled several mental attacks already, and now he was ready to put Fernand on the defensive.

Every man's mind was different. Gune's had been a calm pool, wheras Albert's had been a wall with several large doors. Fernand's mind was a pit of vipers, twisting thoughts, and schemes and plans writhing together. Where Gune's emotions had been schooled, Fernand's were a labyrinth of purposefully confusing and misleading lies. His only strength, it seemed, was to be obscure and obscene.

He is still dangerous. Do not let your guard down.

After sacrificing this much? I would never forgive myself. He will pay for what he's done, and he'll pay today.

The faintest sound came from Dante's left. It might have been a tree rustling or a soft boot, but Dante ducked just in time to miss being hit in the neck with an arrow. As it was, the blade of the arrowhead grazed his temple, and he discovered first-hand the reality of the pain simulators. Dante was amazed when he felt the blood trickle down his forehead.

He quickly recovered and threw himself down as more arrows flew from the cover of a low, broken wall ahead. His own archers retaliated with an arcing volley, and his knights raised their shields to protect their Dante. At the same time, he watched the serpentine mind of Fernand Mondego to see the reaction. Ideas and thoughts flashed quickly, but he caught one before it was too late.

"To the side!" he called without needing to. His knights turned their shields to the side just in time to meet a rush of shadowy figures charging their flank. Fernand's assassins flitted in and out of sight, gaining power from the shadows cast by the trees. The quarters were too close for his archers, so Dante ordered them back, sending the occasional arrow to the hidden assailants behind their wall to keep their heads down.

"Break formation and make a firing lane!" he bellowed as he strode forward and added the might of his own sword to the dancing and whirling assassin fighters. His knights were hard-pressed, but they fell back to his commands, breaking into a pincer that left a clear path for his wizards and the special skill, "fire lance," Dante had assigned them.

Spears of flame pierced the shadows and crashed into several of the assassins not quick enough to get out of the way. Their screams were lifelike, and the flailing, burning forms lit up the shadowy gloom of the sparse forest for a moment before they fell to the ground and lay still. The other attackers, their shadows momentarily gone in the firelight, were exposed, and they fell to the swords of Dante's knights. The assassins faded away, running in a frantic retreat.

Dante whooped and gave chase with his knights by his side. They ran from the woods and into the broken city, where most walls were no higher than Dante's head. More of Fernand's assassins fell to arrows in the back as Dante's archers stopped to fire rushed shots. He let the thrill of the hunt and of imminent victory wash over him as, for a second, he stopped watching Fernand's mind, his need for revenge overtaking all else now that it was so close..

You are undone, the other man's voice was mocked in Dante's head. He realized his folly; he'd done the same thing to the Red League, after all, drawing out the enemy and leading them into a trap. He called his units to ground, but he was too late. Small bombs flew from the surrounding buildings and the resulting explosions filled the space with smoke and fire, a menagerie of shadow and blinding

192

light. It was the woodland knights' turn to scream for the relief of death as they burned, clawing at their clothes, the cruel chemicals layering everything in hellish napalm. Dante clawed at his armor, pulling it off as the sticky stuff nearly burned through it and branded parts of his arm with searing pain.

Small clashes of solo battles rang out in the billowing smoke, and it was only by the leaderboard that Dante knew the fight was now evenly matched. He no longer had the advantage of numbers, and his forces were being beaten back amidst the surprise attack.

The pain was immense in his arm and he fought to gain control of his thoughts once again, in order to direct his units. He split his mind and gave the pain to his other self, so he could focus on the task at hand. Fernand's avatar stepped from the shadows and drew two wickedly curved short swords with skulls gleaming at the hilts. The man was always showing off—always so cocky. He *had* changed. He'd gotten worse.

"Time to finish this," Dante said through the normal channels.

"I've got a surprise for you, as well. The restraints in all the other control pods have been disabled, yours included," Fernand said, stalking around his enemy. "Sometimes a mortal blow will kill a player in a full-immersion rig, but now it definitely will."

With lightning speed, Fernand struck.

194

CHAPTER : 32

Dante pulled his unit back and the blow that would have normally been pushed aside by his breastplate instead cut deep into his already-hurt arm. Pain filled his shoulder as the bio patches registered the hit. He looked in dismay as the special attack did its most significant damage, disabling his own special ability for a period of time. He'd been saving it, but now it was useless.

He recoiled from the strike, but managed to put the pain away in his other self, retaliating with a one-handed low-guard slash when Fernand thought the pain had overwhelmed him. The man only barely parried the attack before dancing away warily.

The next attack came quickly as a thrust of a master duelist, but Dante turned aside. Fernand went with it and spun around behind his opponent. It was at an awkward angle for his knight, but it gave him more than the upper hand. Dante felt a hand on his shoulder and was suddenly thrown through the air to land roughly on his belly. Pain flared throughout his body, and he saw red for a moment before shaking his head to clear it. A rough hand grabbed him by the back of the neck, dragging him up. He was suddenly face to face with Fernand.

"There's only two of us left, now," Fernand said, punching Dante in the gut with his free hand before holding one of his short swords to his enemy's throat, "and that means you're all out of surprises."

"Not quite," Dante said while he gasped for breath. He stared into the eyes of Fernand, even as his mind sought out the man's mental equivalent. "You wanted to know who I was."

He focused all his thoughts and mental powers in a torrential attack against the other man's psyche. He called upon the assistance of the *Monte Cristo* and fed the memory of every tortured night, every hoarded experience of pain he had lived with in the Chateau D'If right into Fernand's mind.

The shock on his face was more than satisfying as he staggered back, dropping his blades and holding the sides of his head as if they'd explode. His face paled, his hands shaking at his side.

"How? Those memories..." His eyes met Dante's, fear thick in his gaze. "Edmond?"

"Yes." Dante let his expression finally show the full measure of his hate.

"You died in prison—I saw the report, myself."

"Do I look dead to you?"

"Not dead enough!" Color rushed back into Fernand's face as he launched a special attack, summoning magical blades and whirling into a storm of cutting swords. His aim was off, though, and Dante was able to defend with his sword, pushing the attack away. He locked his normal blade

196

with Fernand's magical one, grinning when they met face to face.

"That's what you hoped, wasn't it, Fernand? It would have been so much easier if I'd have died, just how it would have been easier to kill the crew of the pirate ship we took."

Fernand redoubled his attack.

"Did you think no one would ask you to pay for your crime? I'm here to put a knife in your back the way you put one in mine."

Fernand swallowed, retreating as he gathered his thoughts, but then his expression cleared. "No, it's impossible. You're an imposter after my company. It doesn't matter who you claim to be—it's only the two of us left, and only one of us can walk away from this. You die today."

The magical blades spun again, but with focus and determination, this time. Dante met him with showers of sparks in the smoky air. Distantly, Dante was aware of other small battles, but neither he nor Fernand were interested in being interrupted. This was between them; he'd always known it would come to this.

"You took years away from me! You took Mercedes away from me! You raised my son as your own!" Dante spat his accusations like poisonous darts, rage powering his strikes to come harder and harder. Fernand was forced back a half step at a time. "It had to be you! Only you would have devised this plan. Villefort only cared about money

197

and Mercedes had herself to save, but you would have betrayed me easily. Why? To save your career? Your reputation? We were friends, Fernand! Friends don't do that!"

"Friends?" Fernand panted from the effort of defending himself. "How could anyone be friends with you? Dante the Blessed! Dante the Golden Boy! Dante, who looked out for everyone above his friends—above his fiancée! I saved Mercedes from you! I saved Albert from a life in which he would always come second!"

"You didn't save them—you sentenced them both, Fernand, because you never put anyone above yourself!"

"And what would you call this little revenge of yours, Dante? Selfless?"

With a furious attack, Dante spun Fernand to the ground, his weapon inches from the man's throat. It was here at last: his enemy on the ground, weaponless, vulnerable, and at his mercy. Rage filled him, drowning out all else.

Fernand looked up at him with cold eyes, too proud to plead, but not too proud to die.

"Edmond, no!" Mercedes' voice cut across the landscape just as he was about to take the final blow. His eyes widened with surprise. She'd entered their battle, but why? Was her husband dear to her, after all?

"For the sake of your own soul, Edmond, don't taint it with revenge." Her avatar looked exactly like her as she glided toward them. "You were never this man, Edmond. Have mercy on us."

No mercy, the ship said in his mind.

"Mercy?" Dante's jaw dropped at the thought of showing mercy now, when his revenge was so close he could almost taste it on his lips. Her eyes were dark pools as she pled with him. Had she pled for his future with Fernand as she was pleading now for his? Jack had accused him of losing his humanity and now Mercedes did, as well. His head spun.

Don't listen to her. Seize what is yours.

He hesitated, only for a moment, but it was enough for Fernand.

The man sent out a psychic blast so powerful that it sent him flying backward. The blast was indiscriminate with destruction sent in all directions. He rolled across the landscape, his vision black for a moment, but he forced his mind to be strong and protect itself. He felt the ship reinforcing his barriers, protecting him from the worst of it.

I felt that, the *Monte Cristo* said. *If you didn't have my protection, I'm not sure even you could have withstood such a blow.*

The thought echoed in his mind as he pulled himself to his feet. A few feet away, Mercedes laid in a limp heap on the ground. Dante felt himself grow cold. Ignoring his own safety, he rushed to her side.

His emotions were so jumbled that he couldn't have said which was most prominent. Fear for her safety mixed with old bitterness and lingering hope. Her avatar was dead—that meant nothing on its own. He forced himself to hope, but then he felt it.

The resonance between him and Albert shuddered with grief as his son mourned. She was gone—gone before he ever had the chance to ask her why she had made her choices. His feeling of loss overwhelmed all the rest until, for the first time in years, his desire for revenge seemed to fall away. Loss hollowed his heart and he blinked back stinging tears—the first he'd cried in more than a decade.

He was cold and numb. It felt almost as if he were watching himself from far away. Fernand strode toward him, his eyes only on Mercedes. The man's face was haunted, drawn, and pale, as if he had watched his own death. He looked small, like he were of no more importance than floating debris in an asteroid field. Dante swallowed. Did it even matter if Fernand lived or died? Did it matter if he was ruined or wealthy? He had wanted so long to make him pay, but now it felt so empty.

Hot and searing, tears formed and fell from his eyes. His world spiraled around him, as if the anchor had been lost, and in a moment of horror, he saw himself standing beside Fernand and the fallen

Mercedes and could no longer see any difference between himself and them.

Mercy. Mercedes had asked for mercy, and it was mercy he would give to her husband. He lifted his sword and killed Fernand's avatar with a single overhead blow, not bothering to make it dramatic for the crowd. If his victory was hollow to him, it should be for them, as well.

CHAPTER : 33

Dante stared at the stars in the distance through the massive porthole on the viewing deck as his ship pulled gently out of her docking slip. The *Monte Cristo* was the only ship he'd ever known who didn't need her Captain at the helm for such a careful maneuver, but then again, the ship technically didn't need him, at all.

I might not need you, but I do find your company educational. This idea of mercy still escapes me. She asked you to be merciful to her husband by sparing his life, yet you used the same word when you killed his avatar.

She thought I would kill him, I think. She didn't realize I only planned to strip him of everything.

You mourn her. It occurs to me that perhaps you didn't want revenge on her, after all.

Perhaps he didn't. His emotions surrounding Mercedes were still tangled and confused. Above all, he felt loss, but for the first time in years, he could remember what they'd had before her betrayal. His memories were filled with fondness. If only she'd told him she was pregnant—if only she'd had the faith to trust him. Perhaps she hadn't known, herself. The hatch opened and Dante turned to see Jack walk through.

"I believe I owe you an apology," he said, still looking at the stars

Jack looked around the lonely observation deck, as if checking to be sure no one else was there.

"You came through for me, Captain, and we're leaving this place whole and together. I think that's enough—we don't need to get flowery about it. Are you done with all of this, now? Can we move on and find a new start somewhere? We certainly have the money to try."

Dante had liquefied Mondego Industries in the days following his win, leaving his entire crew fabulously rich when their shares were drawn up.

"I'm done with it, Jack, but I think that something—between us, at least—needs to change."

"Oh?"

Anxiety colored Jack's eyes and Dante let it sit for a moment before finishing,

"I think, from now on, you should call me Edmond."

Jack laughed, clapping him on the shoulder. "Consider it done. Where're we headed, Edmond?"

"I was thinking Davrini Hacken."

"Well, at least you have the wardrobe for it."

"Exactly."

A shuttle is hailing us, the ship said.

A shuttle?

It's Albert Mondego.

Dante reached out with psychic fingers toward the resonance that was an almost constant

203

buzz, vibrating in tune with his own psychic aura. *Albert?*

He'd never tried this outside the game, and he certainly hadn't in the days following Mercedes' death. When he'd emerged from the arena, the look in the boy's eyes had seared him to the core. He knew that kind of hatred—he'd been seeing it in his own mirror for as long as he could remember.

My mother told me something before her death. I need to know if it is true.

Ask your question.

Can I come aboard?

In answer, the ship latched onto Albert's shuttle, drawing it into the bay below.

"Your son?" Jack asked, looking out the port window.

"Yes," Dante said. He didn't know what he would say to the boy. How would he explain the deception he'd used to destroy his family and future? How would he explain how sorry he was becoming for ruining the life of the only family member he'd had?

"Let's hope he doesn't take after you. I've seen enough of revenge."

Dante ran a hand through his hair. Was that what the boy was here for? He could feel the ship guiding Albert up to the observation deck, moments away. If he was here for revenge, Dante wouldn't stop him. He would never be able to lift a hand against his own son.

204

Is that more humanity talking?

The hatch opened again and Albert entered, his young face tight with determination and his eyes as hard as rocks.

"I think I'll leave you to it," Jack said, nodding acknowledgment before leaving the room. Albert strode to Dante, squaring his shoulders. His eyes were red around the rims and his fists clenched nervously at his sides. The older man swallowed, but kept his posture relaxed. There was no need to frighten his son—he wouldn't stop him from whatever he was here to do.

"You're my father. My mother told me while you were in the Bacarrae game before she..." he paused. "It's true, isn't it?"

"It's true."

"You used me to get to my parents, and now my mother is dead and my father is alive, but utterly ruined."

"Yes." It was the hardest word he'd ever spoken. His revenge was dust in his mouth. Albert drew himself taller, like he was summoning the courage for this moment. Here it was: Dante's fate. "I don't believe in revenge," the boy's voice shook as he spoke. "My mother always said it hollowed the soul."

She'd been right about that. Dante's eyes widened, curiosity and surprise filling him in equal measure.

205

"I think you owe me something, though, now that you've taken everything."

"Anything." The boy could have anything Dante had to give—he only had to ask.

"A chance to get to know my real father." Albert's brown eyes looked just like his mother's when he said, "I'm coming with you. For now, at least."

Edmond Dante's eyes stung, tears leaving hot tracks on his cheeks. He hadn't felt anything like this in so long that he wasn't sure what it was, at first. It was relief, certainly, and wonder, but it was also something more.

Humanity? the ship asked.

In a way, Dante replied. *It's love.*

THE END

ABOUT THE AUTHORS

JOHN GUNNINGHAM lives in the flatlands of Saskatchewan with his wife, two kids and two pure bred shelties. He writes spec fiction and the odd poem when he's not forced into life's necessities of family, day jobs and sleep. He's currently working on several short and novel length projects with an eye towards self-publishing. One project among them a collaborative effort with fellow Canadian Sarah K. L. Wilson.
http://johngunningham.blogspot.ca/

Daydreaming is what **SARAH K. L. WILSON** does best. When she was a kid, her family took long road trips and she spent a lot of time looking out the window and daydreaming stories to entertain herself. Now she writes them down and entertain other people. She find run-of-the-mill stories boring and she loves philosophy, so if you want something different and with a mind-bending twist then look no further. Sarah maintains a robust fan base. Join us.
http://www.sarahklwilson.com

Join our mailing list to receive updates on future projects: http://www.subscribepage.com/r1q3a1

Made in the USA
Coppell, TX
09 December 2024

42081813R00115